**The Bunny Blues**

**Sedona Ashe**

*Cover artwork by Sanja Gombar*

https://bookcoverforyou.com/

Interior artwork by Cauldron Press.

http://www.cauldronpress.ca

A huge thank you to-

Allison Woerner for Alpha Reading.

Maxine Meyer for Copy Editing.

Imogen Evans for Proofreading & Editing.

# THE Bunny BLUES

2

HEY THERE,
HOP STUFF

SEDONA ASHE

# CONTENTS

## Sensitivity Note
## (Spoilers Below!)

This book has a bit of the rejected mates trope in the beginning. However, Ellora will find love with the wolves who are ready to scorch the earth for her. She does not get back with the rabbit shifter mates.

Ellora is forced to bond with the rabbit shifter males due to customs within the burrow. The men do not force themselves on her, but due to the pain of the heat, she is forced to accept their help to ease the pain. They knew that would happen, so they did take advantage of her heat to manipulate her.

The rabbit shifters ignore her until she is useful in furthering their businesses or satisfying their needs. They do not need to take her body by force since she hopes by being the perfect mate, they will fall in love with her.

They do cheat on her.

There is some violence and death. (What can I say? Wolf mates are protective!)

The wolf shifters do come with special equipment upgrades they can choose to use.

# Chapter ONE

## ELLORA

Curling into a ball on my side, I tried to make myself as small as possible.

It was strange that I was trying to avoid being noticed by my mates when the thing I longed for most was their attention. But experience had taught me that although they might notice me, I'd never get the type of attention I craved.

The four male rabbits were happy to answer the seductive call of my heat. And why wouldn't they? The alluring perfume of hormones, the provocative changes to my lips and curves, and the candy-sweet taste of my skin—they were the ways biology made sure my mates couldn't resist me.

I ran my fingers over my skin, hating the way it still tingled from their groping hands. Every muscle in my body ached from the near-feral way they'd pounded themselves inside me. My heat was temporarily satisfied, but my heart lay shattered in my chest.

When the men had finished their "duties," they'd rolled from the bed and dressed. Without a backward glance, each man had left the room and returned to his business as usual.

Young female rabbits were taught about the agony of being in heat and the dangers that came with it. But we were also reassured that our mates would be by our side to help bring us through it, thus creating a stronger bond within the fluffle.

Yep, most female rabbits were blessed with adoring mates who brought them plates piled high with their favorite snacks. I'd even heard of men who, after mating, would carry their female into the bathroom to soak in a steaming hot bath while being gently washed.

Did I wish I could have mates like that? Absolutely. However, I could survive without those tender, thoughtful gestures. Still, I would've given anything to feel my mates wrap their arms around me as I fell asleep in their arms rather than lying alone in an empty bed.

I knew what it was like to have mates who lusted after me, but what would it feel like to have mates who *loved* me?

Edward, Jay, Henry, and Brett had made it clear from the day we were paired that love wasn't something I would ever receive from them. Henry and Brett were too busy pursuing careers as high-powered attorneys.

Edward and Jay's lives had been consumed with buying up every piece of investment property they found and reselling them to clients with pockets deeper than the Mariana Trench. And before we were matched, both men had gained a reputation for having a different cottontail in their beds every chance they got.

A single tear slid down my cheek as I recalled the nightmarish day my world had crumbled around me. When I'd learned these four men were my match, I'd been horrified. They were not the type of men you could build a fairytale life with.

After I'd gotten over the shock, I'd met with the guys, hoping maybe I'd misjudged them. Maybe they were ready to settle down and create a strong partnership.

The meeting had gone exactly how I'd thought it would.

Edward had droned on about the importance of making sure they weren't all tied to one female because if I was infertile, they'd need to consider taking another mate to ensure their bloodlines continued. Did he really think I was so stupid that I couldn't see through his bullcrap?

We both knew that if they claimed me, they would be unable to have sex with another woman. Ever. Their inner rabbits would be faithful to their claimed mate and wouldn't allow the human side to get it up for anyone but me.

I called them out on the lie, but Jay and Edward protested that wasn't the true reason.

Henry and Brett were too focused on their careers to bother with women other than occasionally fulfilling their biological needs. They just didn't want the inconvenience of the mate bond to hamper their travel and work schedules.

According to them, it would be unfair to the company stockholders for them to claim me because their focus would be on me, their bonded mate, instead of their work.

It was yet another lie, and we all knew it. The CEOs of nearly every rabbit-run corporation were bonded to a mate, and they'd done just fine moving up the corporate ladder while maintaining a work-life balance.

When I'd left the meeting, I'd been even more desperate to be released from the match. Rushing home, I'd pleaded with my parents to speak to the burrow's elders to change their minds.

My parents were powerful within the burrow, and if they asked for me to be matched to another fluffle, the elders would've bowed to their wishes without a peep of complaint.

Unsurprisingly, my pleas fell on deaf ears. My parents were delighted with my match—probably because my four mates just happened to be the sons of their closest friends. I'd collapsed to the floor, unable to control my horror and heartbreak.

Instead of pulling me into her arms to assure me everything would work out, my mother had hissed at me to get off my knees before I ruined my dress and embarrassed my family.

Her uncaring attitude to my anguish was like a knife to my chest. But I shouldn't have been shocked. Status and wealth were the only things that mattered to the upper-class rabbits within the burrow... and my parents were no exception.

They then revealed that, unbeknownst to me, my match had been decided the moment I was born. Every drop of blood in my body had rushed to the floor, leaving me lightheaded.

I'd listened as my beaming father explained that the other four leading families had already given birth to sons, and how delighted they'd all been when I was born.

A daughter to bind our families in a close bond.

A mating contract had been signed before I'd turned a week old, making sure the money and power would stay within the five leading families.

It wasn't the elders who had decided my match.

It was my parents.

I'd fought the urge to vomit as my father continued speaking, shattering any illusion that he'd ever cared for me.

He'd known the type of men my matched were. They were cold, selfish, and without room in their hearts to treasure a mate. But my father was willing to let them have their way with my body and destroy my soul—all so he could continue boosting his social standing.

After realizing my parents weren't on my side, and determined to avoid taking those men as my mates, I'd gone to the elders alone and laid out my case. But just like my parents, the elders had dismissed my feelings.

My match to Edward, Henry, Brett, and Jay would stand. The elders rambled on and on about the importance of the matching and how it was a hallowed event within the burrows.

Then they'd warned me I had to submit. If I didn't, I would be confined away from the burrows as they couldn't risk one disobedient bunny disrupting generations of perfect matches.

It was their polished way of saying I would be imprisoned because they didn't want the other unhappy females to think they had a choice when it came to matches.

If I'd had more time, I would've made a plan to escape the burrows. But the overwhelming stress over the matching brought my heat on earlier than expected. I'd been forced to focus on surviving rather than trying to find a way out of my situation.

The decision was taken out of my hands when my mother found me shaking in the bathtub. My skin had been raw and bleeding from where I'd desperately tried to scrub away the scent of my awakening heat.

She'd called my father home from work, dragged me from the bath, and packed my bags. My father arrived home, and they'd loaded me into the car and dropped me off at my matched mates' mansion. With a careless wave, they'd driven off.

To their credit, the four men hadn't forced themselves on me. They'd been honorable and remained in control of their inner rabbits even when the fragrance of my heat was all that could be smelled throughout the mansion.

I wish I could say I'd been strong enough to fight through the pain and need clawing at my body and mind. But I hadn't.

To my shame, I'd given in to the biological demands of

my body. I'd begged for them to ease the pain that was shredding my insides. And without hesitation, they'd eagerly done their best to breed my brains out.

In the brief moments of clarity I experienced during those first couple of days, I'd tried to reassure myself that everything would work out in the end. After all, it was rare for rabbit males not to bond with their matched female.

And so, despite their initial protests, I'd clung to the hope they'd give in to the bond and claim me. They hadn't.

I'd fought against claiming them, but I wasn't strong enough to win against my shifter side while in heat. Thanks to my heat, I was going to be trapped as a mate to four men who didn't care about me... and there was nothing I could do about it.

Everyone in the burrow had heard the horror stories of rabbits who'd been separated from their claimed mate. Within a week, a rabbit would begin to feel the strain of separation.

During weeks two and three, the discomfort would turn to agony. With each passing day, the separated rabbits would be driven almost mad with the need to do anything they could to get back to their mate.

Since my shifter side had claimed the men as her mates, it was too late for me to run. I was trapped here in a love-less fluffle whether I liked it or not.

My matched didn't need me, but I needed them if I wanted to keep my sanity.

And all that had led to me curled up and alone in the

middle of a large four-poster bed in a sparsely decorated room.

Just thinking of the room caused an invisible knife to twist in my gut. It was yet another reminder of how unimportant I was to my new fluffle.

The guys had refused to allow me to create the cozy nest every bunny needed to help ease the stress of the heat. They'd rambled on about the cost of the interior designer, and how I should appreciate the modern, minimalistic style of the home they were providing for me.

According to them, it would be an insult to the award-winning designer if they let me junk it up. I wasn't an idiot.

I knew Edward had been banging the interior designer right up until our match was announced. That was why her feelings about the room were more important than mine.

Their only concession was allowing me to pick three pillows and an oversized blanket to tuck around me.

Grinding my teeth together, I tried to ignore the sound of electricity running through the walls to the strategically placed light fixtures. Every part of my body was overstimulated and on edge, and the incessant noise and harsh light scraped against my nerves like razor blades.

I would've given my right arm to have soft candlelight and happy fairy lights scattered around the room rather than the migraine-inducing white light. But the men had been horrified at my requests and shot them down immediately.

At that point, complete darkness would have been

preferable, but the men had left without bothering to flip off the lights.

Cracking open an eye, I studied the light switch across the room. Desperate as I was, my trembling muscles told me that if I attempted to climb from the bed, I'd end up face-planting on the floor.

Out of options, I pulled the blanket over my head, trying to block out the light and high-pitched buzzing. Under the protection of the blanket, I felt free to give in to the sorrow that was consuming me. Great, racking sobs shook my entire frame as I cried for the imaginary life I would never have.

I'd idiotically hoped the men would soften and they'd find themselves falling in love with me. But that was impossible, since they'd already found their true love—*themselves.*

My heat would be over in a day or two, and we'd return to normal life.

Except my life was forever changed.

My rabbit had claimed these men as her mates, and it was something that could never be undone.

I cried until I was sick of crying.

My life might have seemed hopeless, but I was still alive, and I was determined to make the best of my situation.

Maybe if I was the perfect mate, my mates would fall in love with me. And so, I began to come up with a plan. I'd keep the mansion spotless and filled with the delicious scents of elaborate dinners and fragrant baked goods.

I'd make it so my mates were eager to rush home to me

after work, and they'd never have reason to look elsewhere for comfort or pleasure.

I'd be the perfect mate.

A tiny seed of hope unfurled in my chest. I would make this work.

*I have to.*

# Chapter TWO

## ELLORA

I held onto my resolve through the last two days of my heat, but that didn't keep me from needing to hold back tears while their hands greedily traveled across my skin, and they found their release in my body.

There was no love or feeling in their touch, only carnal lust, and I'd sworn that by my next heat, things would've changed. I was determined to have my mates touch me with love.

When my heat finally passed, our lives fell into a new normal, and I worked hard to be the perfect little mate. I tried to come up with ways to please the guys.

Each morning, I woke before they rose. I would hurry to make myself look presentable so I could rush into the kitchen and prepare their coffee and breakfast.

Yet day after day, the guys scarfed down their food,

chugged their coffee, and headed out the door without little more than a jerk of their chins in my direction. I was left blinking back tears and hiding my sadness behind a brilliant smile. After all, no one wanted to be with someone who cried all the time.

As the days passed, I lost count of the number of times one of my mates would come into my room at random hours of the night to take care of their biological needs. I never refused or complained.

My shifter side was elated at any and all physical contact, but when my mates left my room after finishing, instead of curling up in bed beside me, fresh cracks would appear in my heart.

I murmured no complaints when one of the guys asked me to attend business dinners and act as their adoring arm candy, even though I would've rather stayed home with pizza and a movie. They'd parade me around their peers, and I'd keep my smile firmly in place, sipping my wine and listening to the endless, mind-numbing small talk.

There were times when I sat at the ugly marble dining table, surrounded by my mates and listening to their laughter as they ate the meal I'd prepared, that I convinced myself it was working. They were softening to me, and with time, they'd fall in love.

Tonight was another business dinner, and although I'd felt ill most of the day, I wasn't going to tell Brett I couldn't go. It had taken me twice as long to get ready, but I was nearly ready.

Standing in front of the mirror, I used concealer to cover

the dark circles beneath my eyes. Satisfied that I'd evened out my skin tone, I used mascara and eyeshadow to give my eyes a sultry, smoky look that I hoped would help hide my bone-deep exhaustion.

Emerging from my room, I came face-to-face with Brett, who was leaning against the wall outside my bedroom door. For a moment, I thought he might pull me into his arms and compliment my efforts, but I was left disappointed.

Brett gave me a once over from head to toe and grunted, "That will work. You look good."

Even though my feelings were hurt, the stupid mate bond had me flushing in delight at the utterly underwhelming compliment.

*I hate it.*

"Are you ready to go?" Brett asked, twisting his wrist to check the time on his oversized gold watch.

"Yes. Where's Edward?" Both of my mates were attending the dinner, but I hadn't seen Edward since he'd left for work that morning.

Brett headed down the stairs, speaking over his shoulder. "He'll meet us there."

I started to nod but stopped when I realized he couldn't see me. We didn't speak again as we made our way outside to the waiting car.

I tried to make small talk with Brett, but he was too absorbed in whatever was on his phone screen, so I fell silent for the remainder of the ride to the elegant convention center that sat in the middle of the burrow.

When Brett opened my door and helped me from the car, my heart did a happy flip-flop at the thoughtfulness of the gesture.

*Stop being pathetic, Ellora. You're like a puppy begging for attention,* I chided myself. I used to think I was a strong woman, but the stupid bond was making me weak and desperate to be loved by my mates.

Despite my inner thoughts, I couldn't keep from smiling when Brett tucked my hand into the crook of his arm and led me toward the open doors. This was progress and gave me hope that the mission to win my mates' hearts was working.

For the first time since being matched, happiness bubbled in my chest, and I relished the sweet, non-sexual physical contact with him. The men were fine touching me during sex, but they didn't initiate physical contact outside of the bedroom.

Brett guided us to our assigned seats and pulled out my chair. Two of the women seated at the large circular table watched him. It was clear by the stars in their eyes that they thought he was a man in love and that I was a very lucky bunny.

I fought the urge to roll my eyes. If they knew the truth of just how not in love with me Brett was, I doubted they'd be so impressed.

Introductions were made, and the first course had just been served when Brett stood, greeting a late arrival to our table. "Edward, I wondered if you'd changed your mind about attending!"

I glanced up, nearly choking on the bite of Caesar salad I was swallowing. Edward wore an exquisitely tailored black tuxedo that hugged his muscles perfectly.

He'd decided to forgo wearing a tie and had left the top buttons of his crimson silk shirt undone. Dark, shoulder-length hair fell loose around the sharp angles of his face, giving him the appearance of a dark fae king—or at least what I imagined a fae king would look like without the sexy pointed ears.

There was no denying when it came to raw sexiness, all four of my mates exuded it in spades. Every woman seated at our table looked like they would've given ten years of their life to spend one night with Edward.

How ironic. I had shared a bed with Edward, and I would've traded my life to spend one night in bed with a mate who loved me.

Despite my hurt, I couldn't blame my body for responding with a flush of desire when Edward's eyes dropped to me. He took in my thick mane of blue hair that had been styled into loose, sex-tousled curls. His tongue slid across his bottom lip as his gaze traveled lower, following the neckline of my gown as it plunged between my breasts.

Blood pounded in my ears, and my skin tingled under his heated stare. There was no denying he wanted me, and every woman sitting at that table knew it. It caused my inner self to perform a ridiculous happy dance…

A happy dance that ended the moment a woman wrapped her arms around Edward's bicep.

The raven-haired beauty looked up at him through her long lashes and purred, "Darling, are we going to sit? I'm famished."

*Darling.*

*Darling?*

*Darling.*

The word was stuck on a loop, replaying over and over inside my mind. Maybe I'd misheard? Or maybe she'd mistaken Edward for someone else? That thought was disproved when Edward turned to her with a smile.

He definitely knew her.

The warmth in that smile was something I'd spent weeks trying to earn from him. Seeing him give it to another woman hit me like a sucker punch. The few bites of salad I'd eaten turned to a leaden weight in my stomach.

"Apologies, Clarice. Here, let me help you." Like the well-trained gentleman he was raised to be, Edward pulled out her seat before taking the seat beside her.

Clarice. She was the woman who'd decorated the mansion. While I couldn't deny her taste in men was impeccable—at least when it came to outward appearances—her taste in home decor left a lot to be desired.

It was because of her I'd spent my first heat constantly on edge rather than cozy in a nest.

When Edward threw his arm over the back of her chair, the idiotic beast inside me screamed in pain, but I kept my face from showing any reaction at all.

Why would a rabbit shifter female go after a male who was

already matched? Maybe she just didn't know? Maybe she had been invited to this event months before I'd been matched with him, and Edward hadn't wanted to be rude by revoking the invite? My mind worked to come up with a multitude of excuses to explain away the blatant disrespect being shown to me, but deep down, I knew they were more than friends.

Even if they were no longer sleeping together, they'd been bed buddies not too long ago. And if the furtive glances being shot my way from the rest of the shifter women at our table were any indication, I wasn't the only one who thought so.

By some miracle, I managed to swallow a few bites of each course and managed a bit of small talk. After the meal was finished and the plates were cleared, Brett moved around the room, rubbing elbows with the who's who of the burrows.

I lost track of Edward and Clarice, but it was just as well. I wasn't sure how much more my heartbroken shifter could bear.

The mate bond was a powerful thing. To a human, the betrayal of a partner was gut-wrenching. But to a shifter, it was absolutely devastating.

The men had never promised me love or that they would complete the mate bond by claiming me. But my animalistic side had no way of understanding why her mates were refusing to accept her.

I couldn't blame her. Even with human logic, I couldn't deny the pain stabbing at my chest. The men had been clear that if I couldn't produce an heir, they would find someone who could.

However, I'd been under the impression that after we'd been matched, they had stopped sleeping around and that as long as I provided for their needs in the bedroom, they would remain faithful.

All four men had eagerly used my body whenever they pleased since I'd moved into the mansion, and I'd done my best to make it pleasurable for them. Which is why Edward's flirtatious comments to Clarice and the familiarity with which she touched his arm and chest felt like a betrayal of our arrangement.

It was degrading enough living in a home with four mates who treated me with indifference, but to have Edward flaunt another woman in front of the burrows was a humiliation I hadn't anticipated.

Males who didn't bond with their females were rare, and those shifters were careful to keep their affairs out of the public eye and far away from nosy bunny noses.

"Ellora!"

Turning my head, I searched for the voice and found my best friend, Kacy, rushing toward me.

"Hi—*umpf!*" I grunted as her arms circled my neck, and she attempted to squeeze my soul from my body.

Maybe I was lightheaded from the hug, or maybe it was because her hug was the first affectionate contact I'd experienced in weeks, but tears sprang to my eyes without warning.

For a moment, I felt like someone cared and I wasn't alone in the world.

"Kacy, your friend is turning purple. You should probably turn her loose before you catch a murder charge," an amused male voice said from behind my best friend.

"I've missed your face!" Kacy laughed, finally releasing me from the crushing hug. Then, catching sight of my watery eyes, Kacy's eyes shimmered. "Don't you dare start crying! You'll make me cry, and both our makeup will be ruined!"

Grabbing a tiny cocktail napkin, she carefully wiped away my stray tears and fixed my makeup.

Brett whispered in my ear, "You're making a scene. Don't embarrass me."

A pulse of anger shot through me. *I'm making a scene?*

Why hadn't he told Edward that when he'd been feeding another female from his fork?

Ignoring Brett, I grabbed the unused cocktail napkin from Kacy's hand and dabbed under her eyes. "There, now you don't look like you're about two minutes away from turning into a trash panda," I teased.

The unfamiliar male wrapped his arms around her waist, pulling her back against his chest. "She'd make the cutest little trash panda, though." He hooked his chin over her shoulder and pressed his cheek against hers.

The stark difference between Brett's and her mate's reactions had me biting the inside of my cheek to keep a fresh wave of tears at bay. Kacy and I had been matched to our fluffles the same week, but the difference between how our mates treated us was dramatic.

She was loved.

*I'm not.*

It was as simple as that.

"This is Bray." Kacy introduced her mate, rolling her eyes. "And if he doesn't quit trying to feed me every fifteen minutes, I'm going to be chubbier than a trash panda."

Reaching out, I grabbed her hand and gave it a squeeze. "I'm so happy for you, Kacy."

It was the truth. While I would have loved to have even a tenth of the affection from my mates that Bray was showering on Kacy, I was thrilled my childhood friend was getting the adoration she deserved.

Kacy gushed about her fluffle. Her eyes sparkled as she told me about each guy and compared them to her favorite actors.

While she spoke, the rest of her fluffle appeared at her side, stroking her hair, kissing her cheek, or caressing her arms, each of them seeking the reassuring touch of their mate.

"We need to go. I have two more people I need to speak with before they leave." Brett took my arm and tilted his head in Kacy's direction. "Excuse us."

I let him lead me away without complaint. Part of me was even relieved at the interruption. I knew my best friend, and as soon as she caught her breath, she was going to ask about my fluffle... and I didn't have a clue how to answer.

If we'd been alone, I might've poured out the whole bitter story, but I couldn't risk breaking down in public. Besides, this was the happiest time of my bestie's life—essentially her honeymoon—and I didn't want to burden her with my problems.

With no small effort, I kept my smile in place for the next hour and only let it slip when the car door closed behind me.

Unstrapping my heels, I sighed with relief and sagged back against the leather seat. We rode home in blessed silence, and my eyes drifted closed.

"We're home."

I jerked, startled awake by his voice.

"O... Okay," I mumbled and climbed from the car.

"You did good this evening." A warm glow lit my chest with the praise, but it was quickly doused when Brett motioned toward the car. "Don't forget your shoes. I don't like other people's crap in my car."

Without waiting, Brett turned and strode toward the house, leaving me standing in the driveway.

I was a strong, capable woman, and I could carry my own dang shoes...

But I couldn't help but imagine how differently Kacy's fluffle would've treated her in this same situation. They wouldn't have allowed her to carry a thing, and I would bet money they would have carried her into the house as well.

My jaw tightened in frustration. I loved taking care of my mates, but I wanted to be taken care of too.

*Stop whining, Ellora. This is your life now, and you will get used to it.*

My inner pep talk did nothing to make me feel better. At some point, my disappointment would have to ease, and I'd become numb to the hurt. It was strange how much I looked forward to that day.

Grabbing my shoes, I closed the car door and trudged up the dark sidewalk toward the mansion.

# Chapter THREE

## ELLORA

I shivered as I entered the house. It was cold and empty, nothing like the warm home I'd dreamed of owning as a little girl.

Brett had already disappeared into his office, and the rest of the fluffle was nowhere to be seen. Deciding I was too tired to carry on a conversation, I went straight to my room.

Tossing my heels to the floor, I collapsed onto the bed without bothering to remove my makeup or dress. The moment my head hit the pillow, the blessed nothingness of sleep claimed me.

I wasn't sure how long I'd slept before the sound of feminine laughter drifted through my dreams. It was followed by the rumble of a man's voice. My eyes fluttered open. Was it a dream?

Lifting my head from the bed, I listened. The only sound

I heard was the loud, echoing tick of the ornate grandfather clock that stood at the end of the hallway outside my room.

After tossing and turning for an hour, I fell into a fitful sleep, only to be awakened by my alarm far too soon. The men would leave for work in two hours. I needed to make myself presentable and start making breakfast.

Stumbling to the bathroom, I cleaned the smeared mascara from my face and ran a brush through my hair in a futile attempt to tame it. While I brushed my teeth, I studied my reflection and debated applying makeup in an effort to make myself more attractive to my mates.

Then I remembered their lack of interest the night before.

I wasn't conceited, but I'd looked my best last night, and all it had earned me was a backhanded compliment. If my most glamorous self hadn't attracted my mates, I doubted a dab of concealer and swipe of mascara was going to make a difference.

Deciding I deserved a morning of relaxed comfort, I pulled my hair into a bun and slipped on a pair of comfy sweatpants and an oversized tee shirt.

I paused in front of the mirror to study my reflection one last time. Meeting my dark blue eyes, I hated the sadness I could see swirling in their depths.

"You've got this, Ellora. One day at a time," I whispered before flicking off the bathroom light and heading downstairs to make breakfast.

Less than an hour and a half later, I was pulling a tray of made-from-scratch biscuits from the oven. A strand of hair fell loose from my bun, and I blew it out of my face so I could admire the fluffy, golden yumminess in front of me.

I often wondered where I'd gotten my love for baking and cooking from. My mother never stepped foot in the kitchen unless it was to open a bottle of wine. We'd had a chef who made all our meals and maids who kept our sprawling house spotless.

My parents had been horrified to find me covered in flour and kneading a loaf of bread when I was six. They only spoke to me at dinner, and the rest of the day, I was left in the care of teachers or house staff, so I wasn't sure why they were upset to find me in the kitchen.

Actually, I did know why they'd been upset.

Unexpected company had dropped by, and they'd wanted to parade me in front of them... all to add to the illusion of having a perfect life everyone should be envious of.

After that experience, I'd continued to bake and help Mark, our chef, prepare meals. But I'd been more cautious about staying clean and stayed away from the kitchen whenever we had company.

A grin spread across my face as I thought of my mother's reaction if she knew I'd taken over most of the cleaning and cooking at my fluffle's mansion. I didn't care what she thought; I wanted to take care of my mates.

Footsteps above my head told me the men were stirring and would be down to eat soon. Hurrying around the kitchen, I placed the biscuits on an oversized plate and sat bowls of peppered gravy, three-cheese scrambled eggs, and diced potatoes in the center of the table.

I'd just finished setting the table when their footsteps echoed on the wooden staircase. Taking a deep breath, I made sure to hide any traces of my sadness and forced a bright smile onto my face.

A smile that faded the instant my eyes landed on the woman being led into the dining room on Edward's arm.

Clarice.

Like a punch to my gut, I realized I hadn't dreamed the sound of a woman's laughter the night before. It had been humiliating to have Edward shower her with attention in front of the burrow, but it was nothing compared to knowing she'd been in my home... and in my mate's bed.

"It smells amazing," Henry rumbled, his voice still heavy from sleep.

He walked by me without so much as a peck on the cheek. All four men ignored me, their attention on the table.

It would have bothered me if my body hadn't been turned to stone by the woman acting as though she had every right to be in the house in nothing more than a silk gown.

"There are only five seats," Edward commented, his hand resting on the back of his chair as he studied the table.

"That's okay, I have a seat for Clarice." Scooting back his chair, Henry pulled her onto his lap.

Clarice laughed, and the sound caused my throat to tighten until I could barely breathe.

"She's my guest," Edward growled, sitting down in his seat.

"But sharing is caring." A smirk spread across Henry's handsome face. "Besides, Clarice likes it when we share her."

"Henry!" Clarice gasped in mock embarrassment.

She pressed her palm to his chest, and the movement caused her robe to fall open slightly. All four of my mates' gazes were instantly drawn to the creamy skin of her cleavage that had been exposed.

A tremor traveled through my body, and emotions I'd locked away began battering at the door, holding them back.

I wasn't an idiot. The guys weren't looking at Clarice with love. They were eyeing her like horny dogs with a bone, or more accurately, *boners*.

It was the lust mixed with genuine affection that finally broke me. I was their matched, yet they couldn't be bothered to treat me with a shred of decency.

Once a shifter has claimed their mate, it is nearly impossible for them to fall out of love with that mate, or mates. I'd been hurt countless times by how the men treated me, but my inner bunny had refused to see them as anything less than wonderful. They were her mates, even if they hadn't claimed us back.

Last night, watching Edward interact with Clarice had shaken her, but she'd still believed he would honor the fact we were matched.

Standing in the kitchen, watching our mates interact

with another female while barely acknowledging our existence, was the final straw. We both gave up that hope our mates would ever learn to love anyone but themselves.

These men had accomplished the impossible.

They'd caused my inner animal to fall out of love.

The sobs of both my human and animalistic shifter tore through my mind, releasing a torrent of pent-up fury and heartache.

Lifting my chin, I spoke. "She can have my seat." To my surprise, even with the deluge of emotions threatening my sanity, my tone was flat and utterly emotionless.

Clarice struggled to hide her smirk. "Are you sur—"

"Yes. I freaking hate that table. It's so ugly it could scare the crap out of a toilet."

Was it petty to take a dig at her design choices? *Yes.*

Did I care? *Absolutely not.*

The men began speaking all at once. I wasn't sure if it was to Clarice or me, but I didn't care. Heading down the hall, I made my way to the staircase and back to the safety of the room I'd been assigned to use when not in heat.

My hands trembled with the desire to slap the artwork from the walls and toss the various vases and weird sculptures decorating the mansion to the floor.

With effort, I restrained myself. It wasn't out of respect for my useless oxygen bandit mates, but because I refused to disrespect the artists who'd poured their passion into their creations.

Closing my bedroom door without so much as a whisper, I flicked the lock and rested my head against the cool polished wood. My eyes burned with angry tears, but I didn't have time to cry. I had things to do.

Straightening my spine and taking a steadying breath, I kneeled to pull a large backpack from beneath the bed. The men would leave for work soon, and while I didn't think they would care enough to actually come looking for me, I wanted to get a solid head start.

I didn't know where I'd go, but I refused to sleep under the same roof as these men ever again.

ONCE I'D PACKED my important documents, a change of clothes, cash, and a few supplies, I hired a car to take me to the outskirts of the city that sat just outside the burrows. This was where most rabbit females went to have their hair and nails done and followed up their pampering with hours of shopping.

I hoped that if my mates or parents tried to get in touch with me this morning, they'd think I'd gone shopping. If I was lucky, maybe they wouldn't realize I'd run away until late that evening.

Stepping from the car, I paused just long enough to swap my slip-on sneakers for hiking boots. The last thing I needed was for the driver to remember picking up a girl in beat-up hiking boots from the wealthiest neighborhood in the burrows.

Once I finished lacing the boots up, I tucked my slip-ons into the backpack and lifted it to my shoulders. Thankfully, it wasn't too heavy since I'd packed light, knowing I'd need to move fast.

Spinning on my heels, I headed for the thick woods that lay just outside the city limits. Over the years, I'd spent countless weekends hiking alone through forests all around the region.

If my parents had known, they never would have allowed it. But they thought I was spending those vacations with friends, lounging on yachts or skiing at ritzy resorts in the mountains.

For once, their lack of interest in my life worked to my advantage because they never once bothered to check in on me. Heck, they hadn't even remembered to ask about my trips when I returned home.

The wild beauty of nature was my happy place, and right now, I needed that peace more than ever. My smile grew with each step I took away from the burrows, and the weight of my sorrow began to ease ever so slightly.

I spent the next six hours trekking through the familiar forest and almost regretted it when I stepped out of the trees and onto a paved road. Shading my eyes, I stared into the distance and spotted the hazy outlines of office buildings in the distance.

*Bingo!*

I had done it! Pride welled up in my chest.

I'd navigated my way without marked trails through the woods and came out exactly where I'd wanted to be.

Thanks to the thick woods and the winding roads, I knew this city was a full day's drive from the burrows. But by traveling as the crow flies and not stopping to rest, I'd made it in half that time.

If anyone was looking for me, they wouldn't be looking for me here. Not yet, anyway.

I'd take time to get a good meal, and then I'd cut through the forest that lay on the far side of the city. As long as nothing went wrong, I could put another day's drive between the burrows and myself.

It was a solid plan, but I knew I still needed to figure out where I was going. I couldn't run forever. Worse, unless I wanted to risk the bond driving me back to my cold-hearted mates, there would come a time when I'd need to lock myself away to deal with the inevitable separation pain.

If, by some miracle, that pain didn't kill me, I knew my next heat would finish the job.

Still, I refused to give up on life. I'd been dealt a crappy hand, but I was a thousand percent sure I'd never return to my mates or allow them to touch me again.

I was going to fight until my last breath to find my happily ever after—however brief that may be.

Thanks to my shifter side claiming the wretched rabbit men, I knew finding love wasn't in the cards for me. But I refused to give up believing in myself.

I deserved more.

After hours spent hiking through the woods, it was a relief when I finally reached a tiny pub. Heading inside, I found a dark booth at the back and slouched down in my seat. I'd tucked my vibrant blue hair up in a baseball cap in an effort to keep from drawing attention to myself.

The sweet waitress sat overflowing baskets of onion rings, cheese curds, and fries in front of me. "Your burger will be out soon, honey."

"Thank you," I murmured, waiting until she'd headed back to the kitchen to start cramming the deep-fried goodness into my mouth.

I hadn't made the healthiest selections off the menu, but I'd more than earned the carb overload thanks to my hike that morning. When the waitress returned with my burger, I'd already emptied the basket of cheese curds.

"Here we go." She placed the burger in front of me and then, to my shock, sat down across from me. "I want to show you something, dear."

Ignoring my slack jaw and wide eyes, she pulled her cell phone from her apron pocket and tapped at the screen. Turning it toward me, I stared at the video filling the screen.

It showed a female rabbit shifter.

My throat tightened, and my heart pounded.

"How did you know?" I managed to squeak.

"Because I'm a rabbit shifter too. I'm Bernice. It's lovely to meet you." At my stunned expression, Bernice chuckled. "Honey, with age comes experience. I can tell if someone is a shifter the moment they walk through the door. But I'll admit, this is the first time I've seen a mated female rabbit alone and clearly trying to hide from the world."

Every drop of blood in my body rushed to my feet,

leaving me pale and shaking.

*She knows.*

"Have you looked in a mirror, sugar? You're covered in twigs and mud, and you ate that food like you might not eat again for a while." Reaching out, she laid her hand on my arm and gave it a reassuring squeeze. "I can see the pain in your eyes. You're running like a scared rabbit."

She wasn't wrong about that.

Raw panic clawed at my chest. What if they came looking for me, and she told them I'd been here? What if she reported me to her elders?

"Stop worrying, or you'll have more wrinkles than me by the time you reach my age." Bernice tapped her phone and pulled up another video. "I have to go take another order, but I want you to watch these videos. This Monroe girl might be able to help you with whatever you're going through."

Placing the phone in front of me, she gave my arm a last gentle pat before standing and moving toward a table of men who'd just sat down.

My burger was forgotten as I watched clips of the woman named Monroe facing down her elders with a pack of wolves at her back. The videos had all been posted on Burrowbook, a social media platform for rabbit shifters.

I'd never bothered with social media, so I wasn't surprised I'd missed hearing about Monroe. As I scrolled, I saw hundreds of comments from females saying they wished they'd been able to leave their burrows before they were forced into a match.

There were a few who were disgusted by Monroe's blatant disrespect toward her elders, but those haters were far outnumbered by the women wishing they had Monroe's strength.

I watched the videos over and over, and the thing that drew me the most was the pure love in Monroe's wolf mates' eyes as they watched her. She was their entire world.

My shifter side had already claimed my matched as mates, so that was something I would never experience. But maybe she could help keep me away from my fluffle, my elders, and my parents until my next heat.

Then I would be free from their control... *permanently.*

When Bernice returned to retrieve her phone, I'd made a decision.

I knew exactly where I was going.

Too excited to eat another bite, I placed enough money on the table to cover my bill and give Bernice a hefty tip. I couldn't help but throw my arms around Bernice's neck.

She wrapped her arms around me, and for the first time in my life, I knew what a motherly hug felt like. I committed the precious moment to memory, doubting I'd ever experience it again.

When I pulled away, Bernice patted my cheek. "Take care of yourself, dear. And remember to stop by if you're ever in these parts again. I'd love to know you're all right."

With a last smile, I stepped outside. The edge of the forest beckoned me, and I could barely keep myself from running into the welcoming woods. Now that I knew where I was going, I was determined to get there as fast as I could.

# Chapter FOUR

## BRETT

Pushing open the front door, I stepped into the mansion and took a deep breath. I waited for the intoxicating scent of roasted meats, seasoned vegetables, and fresh bread to fill my nose—except they didn't come.

Glancing around the foyer, I noticed most of the house lights were turned off, and a cold emptiness trickled through the house. I set my briefcase down and loosened my tie as I made my way toward the kitchen.

Turning the corner, I entered the kitchen and found Henry and Edward leaning against the counters. Both men looked as confused as I felt.

The dishes from breakfast were piled high in the sink, a faint dusting of flour coated the countertop where Ellora had rolled out the biscuits, and a dirty skillet sat on the back of the stove.

I'd been looking forward to an elegant home-cooked meal, but Ellora hadn't even started preparing it. My annoyance flared, and my blood pressure rose.

It had been a long day at the office, where I had to deal with an ungrateful boss who barely acknowledged my existence. The last thing I wanted was to arrive home to this mess.

"Where's Ellora?" I pinched the bridge of my nose.

"Not here," Edward answered, his voice tight.

I looked to Henry, hoping he'd have more information.

"You know as much as we do, man." Henry shrugged. "It doesn't look like she's stepped foot into the kitchen since this morning."

"So what did she do with her day?" Anger began roiling inside me. "How did we end up with such a lazy mate? She can't be bothered to clean up this mess? Is it too much to have something as simple as our dinner ready when we get home?"

"Maybe she was upset about Clarice, and she's sulking?" Henry poked at the dishes in the sink before gagging and stepping back.

Edward snorted. "Did you see what a mess she was this morning? Ellora has no right to throw a fit like a child over Clarice. Especially if she can't be bothered to make even a minimal effort with her appearance."

I couldn't agree more. "Ellora needs to learn she doesn't get a say over the guests we choose to have in *our* house. And you saw what she looked like at the banquet. It wouldn't hurt for her to put that same effort into her appearance here at the house as well."

"I'm shocked you didn't tap that before you arrived at the banquet. I'm not sure I could have resisted." Edward licked his lips.

He wasn't wrong.

Ellora had looked like a goddess in the clingy, velvet dress, with her hair falling wildly around her face and so much of her skin exposed for our eyes and tongues to slide across. If I hadn't been stressed about the visiting VIPs attending the banquet and needing to impress them, we wouldn't have made it to the dinner at all.

The only reason I hadn't spent the night finding pleasure in Ellora's body was that Clarice had relieved my pent-up stress in the banquet's bathroom. It had freed me up to focus on work my boss had asked me to take care of once I got back home.

"If I hadn't already invited Clarice to stay the night last night, I would've kept Ellora up all night." Edward echoed my internal thoughts. "We need to have a sit down with her. She needs to know we expect her to put in a little more effort when it comes to keeping up her appearance."

Henry and I nodded in agreement.

"Ellora wasn't in her room or anywhere upstairs." Jay strode into the room.

"That's odd." My brows shot up in surprise. Since Ellora had moved into the house, if she went out during the day, she was home before we returned.

Edward's forehead creased. "Do you think she's okay?"

Henry waved away his concern. "Get real, Ed. She's ticked off about Clarice, I guarantee it. Just like when she stormed out of the kitchen this morning. I bet she's shopping, probably running up the house credit card out of spite."

I joined the guys in laughter, but his words caused something else to occur to me. "Hey, we did give her a house card, didn't we?"

We each shook our heads.

"Huh. That means she's been paying for all the groceries and house supplies herself." Jay sat down on a kitchen stool.

"It isn't like she's broke." Edward ran a finger through the flour on the counter. "Her parents could afford to cover her costs for a few weeks. I bet her mommy and daddy have been paying her bills for years."

Jay's stomach complained loudly. "So, while she's out shopping, what are we supposed to eat?"

Edward moved to the refrigerator and yanked open the fridge. He stared blankly at the contents before slamming the door shut, a hopeless expression etched on his face.

Henry pulled out his cell phone. "Pizza it is."

We each took our seats at the table and listened as he ordered. I scowled and drummed my fingers on the marble table in irritation. Pizza had been a staple meal for us on the chef's days off, but we hadn't needed to order it a single time since Ellora's heat had passed and she'd started cooking.

Without fail, she'd cooked a five-star restaurant-worthy

meal for us every night. Just thinking about the greasy fast food dinner we would be having instead of one of her meals had my anger boiling hotter.

"When she returns, we need to give her a curfew," I grumbled, not caring how ridiculous it sounded.

"Agreed," Jay grunted. "She claimed us as mates. You'd think she'd want to do her duties and take care of us."

"Right? Otherwise, what's the purpose of being matched?" Edward scrubbed a hand down his face.

Henry ended the call. "It'll be here in thirty. Anyone want to watch TV until it arrives?"

Muttering our agreement, we followed him into the living room.

Three hours later, we'd finished eating, but still, Ellora wasn't home. I was barely keeping my temper in check.

"Where is she?" I snarled, pacing in the foyer.

"Maybe she found a date." Jay's smirk vanished when I spun around to face him, and he caught my glowing eyes.

"Why would you say something like that? She claimed us. And that means she's at our beck and call! Even if she wanted to sleep with someone to spite Edward, she can't." I practically spat the words in his direction.

Jay threw up his hands in a defensive gesture. "Chill out, dude. It was a joke!"

"This isn't the time for jokes," I snapped and returned to pacing.

"But just so you know, the claim isn't complete," Jay added, almost to himself.

"What is that supposed to mean?" Edward snapped.

"Well, Brett is trying to make it sound like Ellora would be cheating if she slept with someone else. But she wouldn't." Jay paused, but when no one spoke, he continued, "Her rabbit shifter claimed us, so it is unlikely she'll be able to get her rocks off with anyone else. But since we didn't complete the bond by claiming her back, she isn't fully mated. If we'd accepted her claim and completed the bond, then we would have been a mated fluffle—in human terms, we'd be married."

"So she's in limbo?" Edward asked.

"Yeah. She's stuck because her shifter side claimed us, but since we didn't accept it, it's no different from when a human guy proposes, and the girl says she needs to think about it." Jay scratched the back of his neck.

"So even though Ellora claimed us, she's essentially single?" I was growing more irritated by the second.

"Pretty much." Catching my dark expression, Jay hurried to add, "But I don't think we need to worry. According to what I've read, it's impossible for a rabbit shifter female to give up on her claimed mates, even if they leave her hanging for the rest of her life."

If I'd known there was even the slightest chance she could leave us, I would've found a way to limit her movements. Ellora was our match, and just because we didn't want the commitment of a wife didn't mean we wanted her free to consider other partners.

"Has anyone tried calling her?" Edward pulled out his phone, then paused and looked between us. "What's her number?"

We each shook our heads.

Jay barked a laugh. "I bet we're the first fluffle in history to not know our matched female's phone number."

"Well, maybe she should have given it to us?" Edward pointed out. "Who knows what other secrets she could be keeping from us."

He was right, and when Ellora arrived home, we were going to have to give her some firm boundaries.

"I'll get her added to our cell plan." Pulling out my phone, I sent a text to my assistant, telling her to take care of it the next morning. "That way, we can keep track of who she's speaking to."

"Good plan, Brett." Edward set his jaw. "And we can turn on location tracking, and then we will know where she is all the time."

Henry leaned against the door frame and pulled out his phone for the second time that evening. "I'll call her parents."

Ellora's parents must have answered the phone because Henry moved down the hall to speak to them. When he returned, the angry frown on his face told us all we needed to know.

"They haven't heard from her since the day they dropped her off on our doorstep. Her father reminded me it's our job to keep her in line now."

"He's such a charming man." Edward snorted. "Ellora is lucky to have gotten away and be living with us."

"Except she's thrown our generosity back in our faces," I stated the obvious.

"Well, I have a meeting to plan for, so I can't wait up for her. We can confront Ellora in the morning." Jay stood and headed up the stairs.

Edward stretched and yawned. "Yeah, I think I'm headed to bed too. I didn't get much sleep last night." He wiggled his eyebrows suggestively before following Jay up the stairs.

My anger burned brighter. I'd been eager to relieve some stress with Ellora's body tonight, but she wasn't there. She was probably out at a club with friends and would stumble into the house completely drunk at 2 a.m.

Well, I wouldn't allow it to happen ever again. Tomorrow morning, she would learn a lesson about what we didn't consider acceptable behavior.

I flipped off the outside lights and locked the front door. If she'd forgotten her keys, she could wait outside until we woke in the morning rather than waking us in the middle of the night.

Cursing under my breath, I turned and headed toward my room.

# Chapter FIVE

## ELLORA

Standing on Monroe's porch, I raised my hand and knocked before I gave myself time to get nervous. Where would I go if she turned me away?

I should have come up with a backup plan, but between the anxiety over being tracked and the stress already building deep in my soul over the separation from my mates, it had been too hard to think of anything other than putting one foot in front of the other.

The door flew open, and a giant of a man stood staring down at me. Even though he looked less than pleased at my presence, hope blossomed in my chest. I recognized this man. He was one of Monroe's wolf mates.

"You best not be from the rabbit council. I'm really not in the mood today," the guy practically snarled.

"Um, no. I mean, yes." I'd barely spoken more than a

handful of words out loud since saying goodbye to Bernice at the pub, and my exhausted brain was trying to remember how to string a sentence together.

Monroe appeared from behind the wolf shifter. "You aren't from the council. I don't think I've ever seen you in the burrows."

Not wanting her to see my trembling fingers, I wrung my hands together. "No, I'm not from your old burrow. My name is Ellora. I'm from the Greenbriar burrow in Oregon."

Monroe held out her hand in greeting. "Nice to meet you, Ellora. I'm—"

"Oh, I already know who you are! I bet every bunny in the US knows who you are!" Grabbing her hand, I shook it and smiled.

"What do you mean?" The guy's brow creased. He didn't look pleased, and that worried me.

My smile faded. "Monroe is the bunny who runs with wolves. She's turned our world upside down."

Monroe clutched the door, looking slightly green as though she might vomit.

At the man's questioning look, I continued, "Someone recorded the meeting in the clearing and leaked the video. You were incredible, and I realized I didn't have to accept a role I'd been forced into either. At the end, you told the rabbits they had other options, and they could come to you."

I couldn't resist sneaking a peek over my shoulder and searching the woods for any sign of the men who might be tracking me. "I know you were talking to your old burrow, but I hoped if I could get here, you'd help me escape too."

Tears welled up in Monroe's big, soulful eyes. "Was it your bonded?"

Swallowing hard, I gave a shaky nod. "Except I wasn't able to run before my heat hit. They don't love me. They just want me to give them heirs and take care of their every need. I couldn't stay any longer, so I ran."

Reaching out, Monroe took my hand in hers and led me into the house. "Of course we'll help."

At that, my legs gave out, and I sank to the floor, unable to find the strength to take another step. My shoulders drooped, and I began to sob.

Monroe kneeled beside me, her arms pulling me into a warm embrace. "You're not alone."

"My name is Cillian, and I'm the Alpha. I've already sent a message through the mental link that you are to be protected as a member of the pack. Monroe has been cut off from the local burrow, and that is hard for any shifter, so I'm glad you are here. Please stay as long as you wish." Cillian bent and pressed a soft kiss to Monroe's lips.

He disappeared but returned a moment later with a box of tissues that I happily accepted. "Thank you so much. You have no idea how much this means to me."

Monroe squeezed my hand. "I can't imagine what you've been through since I wasn't bonded before I escaped. But I will do whatever I can to help. You only need to ask."

"Monroe, you've had a stressful day, and you need to recover." Cillian's tone was gentle but firm. "How would you feel about letting Ellora settle in with some of my trusted wolves? She would have more privacy as well."

I wasn't sure what had happened that day, but I could see the fatigue on Monroe's face and the dark smudges under her eyes.

Despite their laughable size difference, Monroe crossed her arms over her chest and faced off with her wolf mate. "She's staying here where I can protect her, unless you have another idea where I can know she is equally safe."

A second male wolf appeared behind her and wrapped his arms around her waist.

"Rig!" Monroe yelped.

"What? You're so cute when you're angry. I just can't resist." Rig nuzzled her neck.

My stomach clenched, and my heart ached at the tender gesture. If I'd found my way here before my heat, I might've had a chance at love like that. At that point, the best I could hope for was safety until my inevitable end.

"Gross!" An unfamiliar female voice startled me from my dark thoughts. "She doesn't want to see all that lovey-dovey stuff. I've already texted my brothers; Coda messaged back that she can stay with them."

Monroe turned toward the female. "Ellora just got here. She might not be comfortable in a house of male wolves. But thanks for the offer, Reese."

"Ellora is going to feel a lot more comfortable with my bros than she's going to be if she stays in the house with you guys. You're practically newlyweds. Heck, as much as I love you, I can only stand so much of the mushy crap before I need a break." Reese shot me a wink, and an unexpected smile touched my lips.

Years ago, my parents had a dinner party for their clients, and a wolf couple had been among the guests. They'd been well-mannered, and honestly, two of the nicest people I'd ever met, but the entire evening, my inner rabbit had been demanding I run for safety.

Bunnies were prey, and the instinct to flee from a predator was nearly impossible to ignore. Hopefully, the wolves' presence would deter my burrow from coming after me since they'd be wary of the wolves, too.

I'd expected to be terrified of the wolf shifters in Monroe's pack but was surprised to find I was only slightly on edge. Red flags waved somewhere deep inside my skull, but it seemed my inner rabbit was either too shattered to be fully aware of the danger we were in or I was too exhausted to care.

If Monroe could learn to feel comfortable with wolves, maybe I could, too.

Cillian rubbed his jaw and nodded. "That's a good plan, Reese. Your brothers are among my strongest enforcers, so Monroe won't need to worry about Ellora's safety while she's in their care. Very few wolves in the US would dare to cross their path, so I doubt the rabbit shifters would risk it."

The wolf, whom Monroe had called Rig, gave a low laugh. "And what does Macarius think of having a houseguest?"

Both male wolves watched Reese with inscrutable looks. Who was Macarius, and why did Monroe's mates seem amused?

Reese rolled her eyes. "Macarius is out of town, so this has nothing to do with him. Coda and Quinten said it was fine." Her phone chimed, and she glanced at the screen. "They want to know if they should head over here now and escort her home?"

"The poor dear isn't going anywhere until after I've fed her. She looks like she might topple over any minute." An older woman bustled into the living room. "I'm Stella."

Not giving me a chance to respond, Stella wrapped me in her arms. The delicious scents of spicy peppers, fragrant onions, and roasted garlic enveloped me.

A fresh wave of tears welled up in my eyes, and I was once again overcome with emotion at something as simple as a hug. It was ridiculous that complete strangers had given me more affection than I'd ever received from my family.

"Don't smother her, Stella." Monroe giggled.

"I don't mind." My face was still buried in Stella's shirt, so my words came out muffled.

Monroe's eyes met mine over Stella's shoulder, and I saw sadness and understanding reflecting in their depths. Rather than commenting on my tears, Monroe grinned. "You're going to love Stella's food. It's incredible!"

My stomach chose that moment to release a ferocious growl, and Stella released me with a chuckle. "We need to get you fed before that beast in your stomach attacks. The food is ready. Everyone to the table!"

A deep blush stained my cheeks, but no one seemed to notice. Monroe linked her arm through mine and pulled me toward the delicious scent of food.

We spent the next hour devouring empanadas, tamales, elote, chile rellenos, and other dishes I didn't know the names of. It was the best food I'd ever tasted in my life, and I prayed Stella would be open to giving me cooking lessons.

Knowing I owed them more of an explanation, I spoke between bites of food. I kept the story simple and to the point, not ready to discuss the full extent of my mates' treatment toward me.

Monroe's eyes had filled with tears as I talked, and when I finished speaking, she cleared her throat. She told me about life in her burrow, about her ill-fated matches, and how the wolves had rescued her.

Every couple of minutes, one of her mates would interrupt Monroe to feed her a bite of food from their fork. Reese would roll her eyes each time, acting thoroughly put out by the show of affection, but the sparkle in her eye told another story. She was happy for Monroe.

The wolves were so attentive to Monroe's every need, and their eyes barely left her throughout the meal. I'd never seen men so hopelessly in love.

Some of my anxiety eased as I sat in the safety of Monroe's home, surrounded by smiling faces. Even so, my muscles remained tense, and I couldn't help but dart glances at the windows.

It had been a week since I'd run. My mates, and probably parents, had to know I was gone and not coming back.

What if they had hired someone to track me? I might have gained time cutting through national park forests those first couple of days, but they could have hopped a plane and quickly made up that distance by now.

Why would they want to put in so much effort, though? It wasn't like my mates wanted me, and my parents made it clear they didn't consider me their problem anymore.

*Pride.*

Neither my parents nor my mates would want the burrows to know I'd escaped. Because of me, they'd be the butt of jokes and the target of wild gossip. My mates would have their manliness questioned, and my parents would face scrutiny for raising a rebellious, disrespectful daughter.

No. They would never allow me to go. And they'd never allow me to get away with causing them embarrassment without punishing me.

My stomach pitched uncomfortably at that truth. It was a matter of time before someone, or several someones, came looking for me.

I'd covered my tracks the best I could by using only cash when venturing into cities for food or supplies. I hadn't even stayed in hotels to avoid further depleting my limited cash and to not risk being caught on security videos.

Instead, I'd found empty holes or fallen logs in the forest to camp inside. Shifting into my rabbit form, I'd back into the stumps, yanking my backpack into the tight space with me to create a sort of door.

It wasn't the safest, but it was easier to camp in my rabbit form than my human form. I hoped my efforts had bought me some extra time, and if I was lucky, perhaps I wouldn't ever be found.

A girl could hope, right?

# Chapter SIX

## ELLORA

We'd just finished clearing the dishes, despite Stella's protests, when Reese's phone chimed.

"I told my brothers dinner was over, so that's probably them." Wiping her wet hands on a towel, she pulled the phone from her pocket and glanced at the notification. "Yep. They're on their way."

Monroe turned to me with a small frown. "I have an idea, but you may not like it."

I couldn't help but laugh. "Lately, my life has been nothing but bad ideas. Lay it on me."

A smile replaced Monroe's frown. "Since you're worried about being tracked here, it might be smart for you to shift to your rabbit form for the trip to the guys' house. We can pack some leftovers in a large cloth grocery bag and stick you inside. The food will cover your scent, so if anyone sees you come inside our house, they'll think you're still here. That way, you can get a good night's sleep without looking over your shoulder every five seconds."

"Beauty and brains!" Rig grabbed Monroe around the waist. Swinging her around, he placed a gentle kiss on the tip of her nose.

Monroe giggled and tried pushing away from him. "Not the time! We're in the middle of creating a plan!"

"It's a solid plan." Cillian stared out the window, appearing deep in thought. "The wolves running security don't know the specifics of our guest, and they know better than to gossip about what goes on at our house to anyone other than the rest of the security detail."

"That gives us time to do some investigating of our own and find out who might be looking for Ellora," Rig added, finally releasing a wiggling Monroe. "But why wouldn't Ellora like it?"

Monroe's sympathetic eyes locked with mine. "Because she'll be at her most vulnerable in her rabbit form. She'll be with two wolves she's never met... while smelling like dinner."

Reese's loud cackle caused all our heads to snap in her direction.

She leaned against the wall, trying to control her laughter. It took her a minute to speak, but finally, she wheezed, "That would suck so hard."

Well, she wasn't wrong.

Unable to help it, I giggled. "Frankly, I'd take being served on a silver platter to wolves while smelling like Stella's incredible food over having my parents dump me on my mates' doorstep while drenched in the sweet scent of my heat."

I laughed harder at the ridiculous mental image, but my amusement faded when I realized no one else was laughing. They were staring at me with wide, horror-filled eyes.

"Are you serious? They really did that to you?" Rig's jaw flexed.

I glanced toward Monroe and caught the slight quiver of her lip.

Hating that I'd upset her, I whispered, "Um, yeah."

"Your parents knew you didn't want the guys as your matched, but chose to ignore your wishes?" Reese clenched her fists.

"It would've been an embarrassment for them if I disobeyed the elders." I interlaced my fingers to keep them from trembling.

"They knew if you were trapped in the mansion, you'd be driven to do whatever you had to in order to ease the pain." A fat tear slid down Monroe's cheek. "They knew you'd end up claiming the fluffle as your mates, whether you liked it or not."

Taking several deep breaths, I worked to calm my tumultuous emotions. "Yes. Exactly. Everyone got what they wanted. Everyone except me."

A fearsome snarl shook the room, causing me to jump. Twisting around, I stared at the two unfamiliar men standing in the doorway. Were these Reese's brothers?

My gaze locked with their glowing eyes, sending a

shiver down my spine. I was in danger... but deep down, part of me liked that thrill of danger. Still grieving the loss of her mates, my rabbit remained silent, but I caught the tiny twitch of her ears in response to their growls.

If these wolves scared us—even though I knew I was a guest in Monroe's home and they wouldn't dare hurt me— these men were perfect to scare away any unwanted visitors from my burrow.

I was willing to suck up any discomfort or unease I felt if it meant having the opportunity to live out my remaining days in peace.

This plan just might work.

"Oh, good! You're here!" Reese squealed.

She rushed to the scowling men and threw her arms around first one man and then the other.

"Hey, sis." The taller guy's face softened a fraction as he hugged her back.

The guy with dirty blonde hair raised a brow at Reese. "Staying out of trouble as usual, I hear."

Reese lightly punched his chest. "Shut up, Quin. You're just jealous I'm having all the fun while you're stuck running border security circles."

The tall guy, who must be Coda, laughed. "She's got you there, Quin." All humor faded from his face as he pinned Reese with a stern look. "But you should be more careful. If you'd been killed the first time Macarius went out of town, he'd never have let us hear the end of it. And we all know he can be a total burro's butt."

The three siblings exchanged a look that made me both curious about, and terrified of, this Macarius guy. A perverse part of me wanted to meet the mysterious man, but the logical part of my mind was relieved he was out of town.

From the corner of my eye, I caught Monroe's yawn and the worried look Cillian sent in her direction. I wasn't sure what had happened before I arrived, but I'd gleaned enough from their comments to know it hadn't been good. They'd seemed reluctant to talk about it in front of me, probably because they saw me as a broken bunny.

As thankful as I was to Monroe for giving me sanctuary, I could see she needed rest. The last thing I wanted was to overstay my welcome.

Clearing my throat, I spoke up. "Monroe, since Coda and Quinten are here, I think it is time I get out of your hair—"

Syrus snickered, but it turned into a cough when Monroe narrowed her eyes at him.

He raised his hands defensively. "What? She said hair. You know, like *hare*?"

Monroe blew out a sigh and rolled her eyes. "Hares and rabbits are two different things. We've already had this conversation, Syrus."

"I know. But it's still funny, Puff." Syrus shrugged unapologetically.

He called her Puff? My heart melted into a puddle of goo. Could her wolf mates be any sweeter?

Another pang of regret stomped on the shards of my

already broken heart. If only I'd run sooner, maybe I would've had a chance to be loved like that.

"Are you sure you don't want to make a run for it while you still can?" Monroe offered, pulling me from my depressing thoughts.

Her features were serious, but her eyes glittered with amusement.

"Yes, I'm positive. I want to stay with your pack, and I swear I won't be a leech! Tomorrow, I'll start looking for a job and will find a way to be useful." I hurried to assure her.

Monroe opened her mouth, but Cillian spoke first. "You will do no such thing. After everything my mate has gone through, it'll be good for her to have another rabbit shifter to spend time with. You are a guest of our pack for as long as you wish to stay."

Syrus was the next to speak. "I already messaged our accountant, and they're setting up an account for you under an alias. It will cover your expenses and anything you need or want." He jerked his chin toward my ragged backpack. "It appears you packed light, so I'm guessing you left a lot of your comfort items and necessities behind."

I didn't want to bring the mood down by telling them I didn't really own comfort items since they didn't fit the aesthetic Clarice had chosen for the mansion.

The unexpected kindness was nearly my undoing. Swallowing the lump in my throat, I whispered a soft *thank you*, knowing if I tried to say more, I'd break down completely.

"Once we've made sure you're safe and not being

hunted, if you still wish to work, we can easily find you a position in a field you enjoy," Rig added.

"I don't know what to say." Grabbing the hem of my shirt, I surreptitiously wiped tears of relief and gratitude from the corners of my eyes. "I don't deserve all this."

Monroe reached out and caught my hand in hers. "We're providing the basics you need to exist. You've been through so much, and you deserve so much more than how you were treated."

Giving me a hug, Monroe stood and shooed everyone from the room to give me some space to shift without an audience.Maybe rabbit's feet were lucky. Because mine had led me to Bernice, and then straight to Monroe's doorstep.

# Chapter SEVEN

## CODA

I paced the hallway and ran my hand through my hair. My inner wolf was usually a chill beast, but since we'd arrived, he'd been whining non-stop, and it was giving me anxiety.

"You all right, Coda?" Quin leaned against the wall, looking relaxed as ever.

I wasn't fooled. He was rubbing a worn silver coin between his thumb and pointer finger. It was something he only did when anxious or stressed.

"Yeah, I'm fine. It's just…" I was unsure how to describe the strange emotions slamming against my heart and mind like a battering ram.

"Same, bro. Whatever this is, it's making my wolf restless and setting him on edge." Quin tilted his head back against the wall and stared up at the ceiling. "Do you think it's the whole prey versus predator thing?"

I paused mid-step. His question cleared the confusion from my mind and sent the unexpected truth surging through me.

A tremor traveled from my head to my boots, and my wolf released a mighty howl that rattled my skull. I got the distinct impression he was annoyed at how long it took me to figure things out.

"Coda?" Quin lifted an eyebrow.

But I didn't get a chance to answer before we were interrupted.

"Guys? We're ready!" Monroe called, but before we could take more than two steps toward the room, Cillian, Syrus, and Rig strode out of Cillian's office.

Crossing their arms over their chest, the three intimidating wolves blocked the hall.

"Alpha. Betas." I bowed my head, and Quin mirrored my movement.

"Before we let you two go into that room, we need to know you'll be able to restrain yourself with Ellora in her rabbit form." Alpha power rolled from Cillian, causing the wood beams inside the walls to crackle.

I didn't dare look up. Cillian was the most respected alpha our pack had ever had, known for being reasonable and for his cool composure. But at that moment, he seemed nothing like himself. He was ready to snap our necks rather than risk letting us make Monroe cry.

As if our alpha wasn't threatening enough, Rig and Syrus weren't any more relaxed. The low bass growls rumbling from their chests caused my eardrums to vibrate painfully. Between the three of them, the threat of violence hung so thick in the air, I could practically taste the bitterness on my tongue.

"Alpha. We were at the burrows when Monroe shifted to her rabbit form and ran among the wolves. Our wolves had no desire to hunt her." I closed my eyes, fighting against the warring desires of running from my alpha or pushing past the three imposing wolves so I could get to Ellora's side.

"But you knew she belonged to us. Most wolves wouldn't dare touch what belongs to their alpha," Cillian rumbled. "So I'll ask again. Is Ellora safe from your wolves?"

If my suspicions were correct, the only risk my wolf posed to Ellora was potentially drowning her in licks and cuddles.

Opening my eyes, I lifted my chin and stared at Cillian. "Yes, Alpha."

"She is safe from my wolf as well. We'll protect her with our lives, Alpha," Quin added.

"Good." The alpha power rolling from Cillian eased enough so I could stand straight once more.

"Monroe would be devastated if something happened to Ellora—or to either of you. But I swear on the moon"—Rig closed the gap between us until we were nearly touching noses—"if you lose control and attack Ellora, I will have no mercy."

When Rig finally stepped back, I found Syrus's glowing eyes were locked on me. "This is your last chance to turn down this mission. We know we're asking a lot of you both. You can say no, and we will find other wolves to guard her."

They couldn't do that! Ellora belonged with me.

*MINE.*

"NO!" I rasped, raw desperation clawing at my windpipe.

My wolf lunged to the surface, stopping just beneath my skin. Every hair on my body stood on end. My canine teeth lengthened to sharp points while my eyes glowed and burned with an intensity I'd never experienced before.

"Ellora is going home with us." I looked between the three wolf shifters. "She belongs with *us*."

My wolf was ready to challenge Cillian if he tried to send her home with another wolf. From the corner of my eye, I caught the bright glow of Quin's eyes and the bulging muscles beneath his shirt. If we were going down, we were going to do it together.

"Huh." The glow faded from Syrus's eyes, and his lips curved into a smirk. "Isn't this interesting?"

"Back down." Cillian's alpha command collided against my will as though he were slapping me with a brick wall, but my wolf continued to struggle against it.

If I'd done this to any other alpha, my face would have been raw and covered in splinters from being dragged across the wood floor as he made me pay for being disrespectful.

But Cillian wasn't any other alpha. Instead of reacting

with another show of force, the alpha power pulsing in the hall faded.

"Coda, Quin. I'm sending her home with you. Calm down." His tone was the same casual one he used on the nights he ate pizza and watched sports with the pack.

My relief was instantaneous, and my wolf backed off without complaint.

*Ellora is going home with me.*

I'd be able to protect her, feed her, and cuddle her...

Syrus's snicker had my eyes darting up.

"What's so funny?" Quin flipped the silver coin between his fingers, a sign he was still on edge.

Syrus stepped to the side, waving us toward the door. "I recognize that look and have a pretty good idea of what's going through your mind right now."

As my brother and I moved past him, Syrus whispered, "If you feel protective now, just wait until you see her in her bunny form."

"Coda?"

I paused with my hand on the doorknob and glanced over my shoulder at Cillian. "Yes?"

"If your wolf ever pulls a stunt like that again, I won't be so lenient." Cillian's eyes held understanding and a warning.

"Understood, Alpha." I ducked my head in a quick bow and then opened the door.

In the middle of the room sat the most adorable bunny. Bright blue eyes that matched the exact hue of Ellora's human hair blinked up at me. The cerulean blue contrasted beautifully against the smoky black of her fur.

Her tiny nose twitched, and my wolf's tail brushed against my mind.

While I stood in awe, staring at her like a weirdo, Quin slid to his knees in front of her.

"Hades!" He scooped her into his arms. "Aren't you the cutest bunny on earth?"

My jaw nearly hit the floor.

Quin, who had a reputation for being an untouchable tough guy to everyone other than Reese, had his face buried in Ellora's plush fur.

Was... Was he giving her belly kisses?

"Hey! What's wrong with you, weirdo!" Reese jumped up, preparing to rescue Ellora from Quin's uncharacteristic behavior.

"Hold on." Monroe held out an arm, stopping Reese. "Rabbits are small, but we can be vicious when needed. Ellora is accepting his attention. If she didn't want to be touched, she would've already kicked the crap out of his face."

We continued to stare at the small black bunny being smothered in cuddles by one of the toughest wolves in the pack.

"Maybe she's just too scared of upsetting him?" When Quin started cooing, Reese looked about two seconds away from barfing. "I'd kill any guy who kissed my belly like that in my human or wolf form."

Monroe laughed. "You have a lot to learn about rabbit

behavior. Ellora is completely relaxed, not tense. She's enjoying his attention."

I studied the beautiful smoke-furred bunny my brother was hogging. Monroe was right; she seemed to be leaning into his touch. When Quin's cheek brushed against her face, Ellora's blue eyes fluttered closed as though savoring the contact.

Still, he could have shown a little more restraint. She was going to think we were insane.

Kneeling beside Quin, I extracted Ellora from his hold, despite his complaints. His eyes glittered with threats of the violence he was planning to inflict on me the next time I slept, but I ignored him. We were evenly matched, and I was more than willing to fight him over Ellora.

I sat the bunny on the floor in front of me. Unable to resist, I stroked my finger against her soft cheek before resting my hands in my lap.

"I apologize for my brother's…" Pausing, I smacked his hand away and ignored his warning growl. "Weirdness. I swear we aren't absolute freaks."

"Speak for yourself." Quin's voice was low and husky.

Ellora's ears angled toward him as though she was drawn to the sound.

I sighed. "Ignore him. Would it be okay if I held you? My wolf is begging me to touch you." Everyone in the room probably heard the strain in my words.

It couldn't be helped; I needed to touch her, or I thought I might lose control of my wolf.

Ellora hopped forward, resting her tiny front paw on my

knee. My heart nearly exploded at her overwhelming cuteness. I gently lifted her from the ground and tucked her into the crook of my arm.

Stroking my fingers down her back, I caught my breath at how soft her dark fur was against my skin. "I feel like I'm petting a cloud."

Snickers came from somewhere in the room—probably the alpha and betas—but I didn't care. Nothing mattered to me except the sweet bunny in my arms.

Ellora's muscles relaxed, causing my wolf to prance around with pride. She trusted us.

Quin shifted positions so he was close enough to run his fingers along the velvet of her ear. "Her fur is the same color as our wolves."

"I hadn't realized it, but you're right." Her hair was a soft dove gray at the base that darkened as it moved up the hair shaft until it turned a dark black at the tip. It gave her fur a beautiful smoke-like ombre effect... Just like my brother's and my fur.

"You're so beautiful, Ellora," I whispered.

The tiny rabbit in my arms trembled, and I winced, worried I'd overstepped. My concerns faded when she snuggled against my chest.

"Awww," Quin and I cooed in unison.

Loud gagging came from the doorway, and I jerked to look over my shoulder. Reese was bent over, pretending to vomit.

"Seriously, sis?" Quin grunted.

Reese straightened and walked toward us. "Well, excuse

me for having a weak stomach. Today was weird, but the last thing I expected to see was my two bad boy brothers fawning over a bunny—a seriously cute bunny—but still." She affectionately smacked the back of our heads. "What happened? You two have turned down every woman who worked up the courage to invite you out on a date!"

*They weren't Ellora.* I kept the thought to myself, choosing to remain silent.

"Leave them alone, Reese." Monroe laughed. "I'm happy to see Ellora will be safe with them. Their wolves don't appear to want to eat her."

"Oh, I don't think it is the wolves who want to eat—" The rest of Syrus's words were unintelligible, thanks to Monroe's hand over his mouth.

But the wink Syrus sent my direction made it clear he knew what was up with Quin and me.

We were saved from further teasing by Stella, who bustled into the room with a large cloth shopping bag.

"Here we go! I packed plenty of leftovers so the poor thing can eat a snack later." Stella eyed my brother and me. "I also packed enough so you boys will be well-fed and not tempted to nibble."

"Oh, they are definitely tempted to nib—oof!" Syrus grunted as Monroe's elbow connected playfully with his ribs.

Ignoring the beta, Quin reached out and took the bag from Stella with a murmured thank you.

We weren't idiots. Stella's food was well known in the pack, and there was no way we'd turn it down.

Ellora yawned, and her tiny nose twitched.

I stood slowly, trying not to jostle her. "I think we should go. Ellora needs rest."

Stopping at my side, Quin held open the bag. With a sigh, I reluctantly lowered the black furball into it. Once Ellora was settled, Quin lifted the bag to his shoulder, and with a nod in the alpha's direction, he headed outside.

"Thanks, bro!" Reese threw her arms around my neck.

Chuckling, I hugged her back. "Always happy to help."

Reese lowered her voice to a whisper. "If you hurt the bunny, you know the alpha will kill ya, right?"

I glanced over her shoulder at the alpha and betas who watched me. They'd obviously heard her whisper. Cillian's arm tightened around Monroe's waist, and Rig stood just behind the pair, running a finger across his throat in a warning gesture.

"No one is going to hurt Ellora," I assured Reese while maintaining eye contact with the alpha and betas.

"Good, because family meals will be awkward if it's just Macarius and me." Reese released me and stepped back.

"That's the truth." I chuckled, and with a wave, I headed outside and hurried to catch up with Quin.

We were lucky Macarius was traveling. He had raised us after we lost our parents, and he was known for pretty much disliking everyone. Heck, sometimes I thought he only tolerated us because we were blood.

When we'd been in school, Quin, Reese, and I had always hung out at our friends' houses because we knew bringing strangers into the house—his personal space—was something he'd never allowed. Reese had been brave enough to try sneaking a boyfriend into her room a handful of times, and I believe the only reason she was still alive was because he had a soft spot for her.

So yeah, it was a massive relief that Macarius was traveling and not due back for a while.

But it was only putting off the inevitable since we were still going to have a problem when he returned... Because whether he liked it or not, Ellora was a treasure. And I never planned to let her go.

# Chapter EIGHT

## ELLORA

Any sane rabbit would have been too on edge to sleep in an unfamiliar house with two predators, but apparently, I wasn't sane. Because by the time Quin lifted me from the cloth bag, my eyelids were heavy, and I was fighting to stay awake.

Quin leaned against the counter, cradling me against his chest while Coda removed the plastic containers filled with food from the bottom of the bag.

"It looks like she needs sleep," Coda commented, opening the refrigerator door and placing the food containers inside. "I can give up my room and sleep on the couch if she wants to rest in there."

Coda's words were directed toward Quin, but he watched me for a reaction. The reaction I could manage was a soft grunt of displeasure.

I wanted to stay right there, cuddled in Quin's arms and savoring the heat radiating from his body. Unfortunately, the only way to voice what I wanted would be to shift back, and frankly, I was too exhausted to work up the energy needed to switch forms.

Although, let's be real. Even if I could've shifted, there wasn't a chance I would have found the courage to tell these men I wanted to be snuggled. It didn't matter that I felt safe in Quin's arms or how content I'd felt with Coda's face buried in my fur. Despite the weird closeness I felt to them, they were strangers.

"Why should she get to sleep in your bed?" Quin's chest vibrated with displeasure. "I know what you're trying to do, and it isn't cool."

Quin's fingers traced along the length of my ear, causing me to yawn and my eyelids to droop lower.

"Stop being an idiot, Quin," Coda snapped.

Was it just me, or did he sound a tad bit defensive?

Quin barked a laugh. "You want her to sleep in your bed so her scent will be in your room."

Cracking open an eyelid, I peeked at Coda and caught the tinge of red on his cheeks. He was trying to look anywhere but in our direction. Oh yeah, he was definitely acting sus.

The wheels in my mind turned at a snail's pace, slowly processing Quin's words.

Why on earth would he want to do that?

"You're only arguing because you want the same thing!

We're both fighting the need to roll in her scent, so you can stop with the innocent act!" Coda snarled.

Without hesitation, Quin retorted, "Yeah, and so what if I do?"

*Back the truck up…* They both wanted me to sleep in their beds? They wanted to roll in my *scent?* Was this normal for wolves, or was there something a little bit wrong with these two?

There was only one reason a rabbit shifter would have for rolling around in the sheets that smelled of another shifter. They were mates.

But Coda and Quin weren't my mates, and they were wolves. So why would they want to wallow around in my scent?

A far more obvious reason popped into my mind and sent an icy-hot shiver of fear racing along my spine.

They were predators, and I was prey. *DUH.*

Respect for their alpha and Monroe was keeping them from eating me, but maybe they wanted to savor my scent while dreaming about eating Hasenpfeffer.

Yep. That had to be it.

I should've been more freaked out, but honestly, as long as they didn't eat me in real life, I figured they could daydream about it all they wanted. It was a cheap, yet weird, price to pay for the safety they were providing me.

Daydreams were harmless and healthy, right? They could imagine what I would taste like, while I imagined what it would feel like to run my hands down their naked—

*Whoa, girl!* I scolded myself and shook my head to clear away the NSFW images. Those thoughts were a recipe for disaster, and the last thing I needed was more man trouble.

Realizing I'd missed the brothers' conversation, I focused my attention back on the arguing pair and fought to open my eyes again.

"Agreed! But how do we know what she wants?" Exasperation dripped from Quin's words, and his arm twitched around me.

"Are you hard of thinking? We ask her." I couldn't see Coda's face, but I was fairly sure I heard his eyes rolling to the back of his head.

"I might not be as smart as you, but at least I'm sexier," Quin mumbled under his breath.

Without another word, Coda took me from Quin's arms and carried me into the living room. Just like with Quin, my body relaxed against Coda. When I wasn't so tired, I'd need to figure out why they elicited this reaction. My rabbit should've been protesting the touch of men who weren't her mates, but she remained quiet.

Coda lowered me onto the plush suede-covered couch before squatting down in front of me. "Ellora? I can't imagine the stress you're under right now, but please know that despite our caveman-like behavior, we don't want to make you uncomfortable."

I was unable to speak, but longed to ease the lines of worry on his face. Summoning the last of my energy, I scooted forward until I could nuzzle the hand he rested on the couch.

Coda sucked in a breath and slid his thumb across the fur of my cheek.

"Why is she so cute?" Quin whispered, walking into the living room.

His arms were piled high with fluffy pillows and thick blankets—far more than one person needed. What were they up to?

"Ellora." Coda drew my attention away from where Quin had begun spreading the blankets on the plush carpeted floor. "We aren't sure where you would feel most comfortable sleeping. You're more than welcome to stay in my room or Quin's room. That way, you can lock the bedroom door to feel more secure."

Pausing, he ran his thumb across his bottom lip. I tilted my head, knowing there was something more he wanted to say.

Quin saved Coda from his struggle. "Or you can sleep here with us."

My eyes snapped to Quin who was reclining on the pile of blankets and my mouth became drier than an Arizona desert. He licked his lip and ran his fingers through his hair giving it that messy, I-just-had-sex look.

"Please don't freak out. This whole situation is unusual." Coda brushed my puffy cheek with his fingertip. "It's just that..." Coda hesitated again, pinching the bridge of his nose.

I tilted my head and waited.

"Our wolves are attached to you," Quin stated bluntly.

"Quin! Why would you say that? Now you've definitely

made it weird!" Coda sat back on his heels and glared at Quin.

"Because it wasn't already weird? Don't you think it's better if she knows our wolves are acting strange because they want to be close to her rather than worrying they want to play with their next meal?" Quin tucked his arms behind his head and stared Coda down.

At least, I think he was staring at Coda.

I couldn't be sure because when Quin lifted his arms, his white T-shirt had ridden up and left me mesmerized by his exposed skin. A thin line of hair trailed down his tan skin before disappearing into the band of his sweats.

My body warmed, and if I'd been in human form, the heat would have no doubt turned my skin as red as a ripe tomato.

There was no way I could deny I was attracted to them, but my mind was struggling to accept it. My inner beast had already claimed four mates, so I shouldn't be feeling anything about these men.

While my bunny wasn't pushing to mount him and ride him like a rodeo-winning bull rider, she was definitely drawn to them. With no small effort, I pulled my eyes away from Quin's treasure trail.

Coda was looking at me expectantly, and I mulled over the situation for less than ten seconds. I knew what I wanted, and my bunny felt the same.

We both liked the idea of stretching out on the pile of blankets between the pair of wolf shifters. Not to mention, the thought of sleeping alone on a cold bed in an unfamiliar house sounded far less appealing.

Unable to tell them what I wanted verbally, and too exhausted to shift, I dragged myself to the edge of the couch and plopped onto the floor.

Ignoring my aching muscles, I slowly hopped across the blankets toward Quin.

As I neared him, I paused and stared at him, my whiskers twitching. I longed to squish myself against him and enjoy the comfort of his body heat, but I didn't have the right to ask for that.

Or did I? The brothers had been kind of fighting over me earlier, hadn't they?

Moving his arm from behind his head, Quin created a space just big enough for me between his body and bicep. Too tired to spend any more time worrying over my body's odd reaction to him, I hopped into the space and flopped onto my side.

Quin rolled to his side, tucking my tiny body against his chest. "Sleep well, Ellora."

The lights dimmed, and a moment later, Coda settled on his side, facing us. His finger trailed down my side. "You're guarded by wolves, and if anyone dares come tonight, we'll rip them to shreds."

I was a bite-sized midnight snack tucked between two of the pack's scariest wolves. Any rabbit in my position would have had the cocoa puff-shaped crap scared out of her. But I'd never felt safer.

My nose twitched in happiness, and the last thought that ran through my mind before I drifted into the best sleep of my life was that I finally knew what it felt like to be snuggled in a nest.

THE NEXT DAY and a half were a blur. Each time I awoke, I was cuddled against one of the brothers.

Rather than trying to rip me to ribbons, the two handsome wolves had lost control and very nearly smothered me in cuddles. It was the most physical contact I'd had since my parents had decided I was too old to have a nanny and had let mine go.

When they weren't cooing over my fur-covered feet or stroking my ears, they were plying me with bunny-sized snacks from a tray they kept filled with treats. They'd even stocked it with water bottles they would pour into a porcelain cereal bowl for me to drink from.

Based on the way they were pampering me, the brothers would make fabulous pet owners, and I made a mental note to tell them that whenever I worked up the energy reserves to shift again.

For the umpteenth time, I opened my eyes. Confusion muddled my mind when I found the room was completely dark. It seemed like it should be morning, but maybe I was wrong, and it was still the middle of the night.

Coda shifted beside me, and the hazy darkness lifted. Blinking away the sleep from my eyes, I stared up at the wolf standing over me.

No wonder I'd been so toasty warm and comfortable! I'd been buried beneath his thick, wolfy fur. After this, I was going to recommend that every girl should try using a wolf as a body pillow at least once in her life, because it was absolutely incredible.

I stretched, then grunted as a dull ache ebbed through my muscles and coiled like barbed wire around my heart. Crap!

I knew this was just the beginning of the pain that came from being separated from my mates, and I'd been doing my best to stuff it into a bottomless junk drawer in my mind, hoping I could forget about it.

Grinding my teeth together, I fought to keep my frustration and anger from consuming me. I couldn't help but feel betrayed by my body's weakness in grieving for the pathetic pieces of trash who were my matched.

Why couldn't I be stronger? I'd done the impossible and escaped them, so why did my body have to keep reminding me?

Coda whined, nuzzling me with his snout, and my survival instincts flared to life. Every muscle in my body tensed, preparing to bolt for safety. But a heartbeat later, my inner rabbit, who'd been lethargic since our heart had been shattered in the mansion's kitchen, stirred.

Rather than being afraid, she was intrigued by Coda's

behavior. With a start, I realized what she'd already figured out. He was checking me for injuries.

Coda was worried about me.

Instead of tightening my control on my bunny, I let go. Curious to see what she would do, I allowed her to take over.

She immediately rolled us onto our back, giving Coda full access to our belly. It didn't seem like a wise move, since he could disembowel us with a single bite, but I held still.

The wolf's warm breath ruffled my fur, and my rabbit responded with a playful kick of her back legs against his snout. I began worrying about her sanity since it seemed like she was trying to get us eaten for breakfast… and not in a fun way.

Coda yanked his head back and sneezed. Resisting the urge to run, I continued to let my rabbit take the lead. She continued to lie on her back and watch him as he tilted his massive head and stared down at us.

Cautiously, he lowered his snout until his nose touched my belly again. For a moment, neither of us moved. Then, to my shock, his long tongue darted out and licked nearly my entire face in a single go.

*What in the carrot frond tickling bull testicles was that?*

When Coda touched his nose to mine, I did the logical thing.

I licked him back.

The dark wolf gave a chuffing sort of laugh, seemingly amused by my act of defiance.

He didn't know it yet, but the joke was on him. Clearly, he had no idea how dangerous bunnies could be!

I was so focused on planning my revenge, I didn't even see his attack coming.

# Chapter NINE

## ELLORA

One minute, I was teasing the massive wolf, and the next, I was being attacked by his long, happy tongue.

Coda ran his tongue the length of my furry belly, up my face, and down the length of my ears. Heck, the wolf even took a nibble of my puffy black tail.

I squealed and shrieked under the wet assault. My shrieks must have alerted Quin to what was going down, because a second black wolf thundered down the hall. Quin bounded onto the carpet and onto our makeshift bed.

If I'd expected him to rescue me, I would have been sorely mistaken.

Instead, Quin gave me a wolfy grin and began lapping at my fur alongside his brother. What kind of weirdo brothers did Reese have?

I kicked and squealed, but if I'm being honest, neither my rabbit nor myself made any real efforts to escape.

I'd spent over twenty-four hours being snuggled and fed by the pair of dark wolves, and it had left me craving more. The past months, I'd been starved of affection, and I was going to take whatever was offered me... even if it came in the odd form of sloppy wolf kisses.

I'm not sure when it happened, but the wolves' playful huffs turned to rumbling growls. Their licks slowed and took on a serious edge.

My heart banged around my chest like a drunken bird at the change in their demeanors, and I worried they'd gotten a taste and might take a bite any minute.

"Whoa! Guys! Have you forgotten I'm not actually prey?" is what I tried to say, but since I was still in my rabbit form, it came out as a string of panicked squeals.

Crap! Instead of calling them off, I'd basically turned myself into a doggy squeak toy.

The tension between the pair of wolves gained strength until it finally snapped. Coda snarled, baring his sharp, white teeth at Quin.

Quin responded by shoving hard against his brother's shoulder. Coda stumbled back a step, and Quin used that to his advantage by stepping over me and blocking Coda from getting to me.

My gaze darted between the two wolves, noting with trepidation the raised hair along their spines and the way their eyes began to glow as they stared each other down. Red flags waved wildly in my mind, and I didn't need to be a wolf expert to recognize the signs of an impending fight.

The good news was their attention was on each other, not me.

The bad news was they seemed to have forgotten I was there, and if they started fighting, I was going to end up flatter than three-day-old roadkill.

The muscles along their haunches rippled, and I slowly rolled to my feet. When the two wolves launched themselves at each other, I was ready. Dodging claws, I darted between their legs with the skill of an agility dog speeding through the weave poles.

No sooner had I cleared the pile of blankets than Coda's dark wolf leaped over my head. Crouching low and keeping me tucked under his body, he spun around to face Quin.

*Carrot fronds!* Did these two doofuses think they were protecting me *from each other?* I'd gone from being ignored by my matched, to meeting my death under the paws of overly protective wolves.

Quin snapped his jaws and released a warning snarl that had my hair standing on end like I'd been electrocuted. He was dangerous, but peeking up at him from beneath Coda's thick belly fur, I felt a sharp pang of desire rather than fear.

That settled it. I was one twisted bunny.

Quin launched himself at Coda, but Coda was ready. With a gentle but swift swipe of his massive front paw, I was sent sliding across the hardwood floor.

I tried to get traction on the polished floors, but it was

futile, and I ended up looking like a cartoon character running uselessly in place. It wasn't until Quin's wolf sank his teeth into Coda's shoulder and sent him sailing into the wall that my tiny claws caught the edge of a wooden floorboard.

Kicking hard with my back legs, I found myself skidding across the floor with all the grace of a first-time ice skater. Coda's wolf shook off the blow and rushed toward Quin.

This time, it was a swift nudge from Quin's wolf that sent me spinning across the floor and sliding beneath a cabinet. Cowering among the dust bunnies that had gathered in the tight space, I watched a battle scene from a nature documentary play out in front of me.

The house trembled as the couch was flipped over, and Quin's body smashed into the large flat-screen TV. Several pictures crashed to the floor, where their expensive-looking frames splintered beyond repair.

When the two wolves barreled into the cabinet I was hiding beneath and knocked it to the ground, I was left scrambling for cover once again. I dodged between legs as the fight continued to intensify.

They had shown no signs of stopping, and I doubt much of the house would have survived if it hadn't been for the front door swinging open to reveal the largest man I'd ever seen.

"What is going on here?" Even though the newcomer didn't raise his voice, it radiated authority.

His voice was smooth as honey, and sent a pleasant

warmth rushing through me. Coda and Quin froze in place, their eyes widening as they studied the giant of a man.

The new guy's attention landed on where I cowered under a couch cushion. "What have I told you about bringing pets into the house?"

The pair of wolves shared a quick look that communicated something I couldn't understand. A moment later, they burst into action.

Quin's wolf spun around and used his body to block me from the man's glowering face. And before I could blink, Coda's snout shoved away the pillow, and his powerful jaws clamped around me.

I could do little more than squeak in shock as he practically flew down the hall. Skidding into a bedroom, Coda used his back leg to kick the door closed behind us and gingerly dropped me on the hardwood floor.

While I appreciated that he'd kept his ridiculously sharp teeth from sinking into my tiny rabbit body, I was beyond ticked off. I'd gone from being the rabbit males' live-in servant to being nothing more than a doggy chew toy.

Fueled by fury, the moment my paws hit the floor, I shifted to my human form. "What in the crispy-finger-licking-Kentucky-fried-frick is going on?" I demanded, crossing my arms across my chest.

Why did he have to be so much bigger than me, even in my human form? Refusing to be intimidated, I glared up at the wolf standing over me.

Coda shifted to his human form, crouching partially over me. "I'm so sorry, Ellora." Regret filled his eyes. "I don't know why Macarius is home early. Quin and I thought it would be easier to explain things to him if you weren't in the same room."

So the guy who could get people pregnant with nothing more than his sexy voice was the infamous Macarius? *Interesting.*

But if he was home from his trip early, what would that mean for me? I'd probably need to find somewhere else to hide from my burrow.

The thought of leaving Quin and Coda had my stomach twisting itself into knots.

"If you get my stuff, I'll leave now," I whispered, hating the hitch in my voice.

"Absolutely not." Coda caught my jaw in his palm and tilted my chin up to meet his eyes. "You aren't leaving us... me."

It was the first time he'd touched my human skin, and my pulse quickened.

That was the horrifying moment I remembered I was in my human form... which meant I was completely naked... and I wasn't the only one.

I was in a sitting position facing Coda, with my legs together and my knees pulled up a bit toward my chest. Coda crouched over me just as he had in his wolf form. He straddled my legs and was leaning over me slightly. His left palm was flat against the floor near my right hip, while his right hand still cupped my cheek.

"It... It isn't fair for Macarius to be forced to share his house with a stranger he didn't invite." My words came out as little more than a breathy whisper, thanks to the intimacy of our current position.

Coda's eyes dropped to my mouth, and the rough pad of his thumb brushed my bottom lip. "I'm desperate to kiss you."

I knew their wolves were fighting over whose room I was going to sleep in when they first brought me home, but just a few minutes before, they'd seemed to be fighting over who got to eat me.

Having Coda the man admit he wanted me was a completely different thing. It was more intoxicating than the finest liquor.

"Then kiss me." The pounding in my ears grew impossibly loud as I held my breath and waited to see what he would do.

A faint glow lit his eyes, letting me know his wolf was near the surface. I'd thought he might crush his lips to mine and take what he wanted from my mouth. But he didn't.

Coda took his time, closing the gap between us as though we had all the time in the world and as though we couldn't hear the muffled sound of his brothers arguing in the living room.

The first touch of his lips against mine was as soft as the brush of butterfly wings. How could something so simple be the most wildly erotic thing a lover had done for me?

Coda caught my bottom lip between both of his, gently sucking and tasting my mouth. My arms slid around his neck, and he responded by sliding his right hand into my tangled mane of hair. He gently lowered me until my bare back pressed against the cold floor.

Bracing himself on his elbows, he kept his body from touching mine. His attempt at being respectful was sweet, but my flushed skin ached with the need to be touched by him.

Tightening my arms around him, I pulled him closer while at the same time arching my back so that our skin pressed together.

The skin-to-skin contact was even more incredible than I'd imagined, and I whimpered into his mouth.

Coda broke the kiss. "Am I hurting you? We can stop."

Instead of responding, I pressed my lips to his.

With my matched, their kisses tended to turn rough rather quickly. The kisses never lasted long before they were thrusting themselves inside me.

During my heat, that had been fine, since I'd only cared about easing the pain. But once my heat had ended, I'd longed for intimacy and foreplay.

In contrast, Coda's kiss remained gentle and unhurried, as though he wanted to spend the rest of the day worshipping my mouth.

*What if this is the closest I will ever come to knowing what it's like to be loved?* That thought stirred me into action and, driven by a newfound urgency, I planned to soak up whatever this man was willing to offer me.

When his mouth moved to trail kisses down my throat, I whispered, "Can I touch you?"

"Yes." The gravel in his voice caused butterflies to take flight in my stomach.

Loosening my legs, I let Coda lift himself off me a couple inches. Bracing himself on his forearms, Coda remained quiet as I rested my fingertips on his chest and began to explore his body.

He was muscular, but not like he spent endless hours in the gym. No, his body looked as though it had been strengthened through hard work and hours running the pack borders.

When my fingers brushed his lower abs, Coda's breath hitched. Worried I'd gone too far, I quickly pulled my hands away and rested them on my stomach.

"Sorry." I turned my head, not wanting to meet his eyes.

"For driving me wild?" Coda kissed my neck. "Please don't stop."

When I didn't move to touch him, Coda shifted his weight to his right arm, so he could wrap the fingers of his left hand around my right wrist.

"You don't need permission to touch me." He gently placed my hand against his stomach. "I'm yours to do with as you want."

It almost sounded like he was saying he was mine forever, not just for a quick romp in the sheets—or in our case, on the floor.

Lifting my eyes to his, I sucked in my breath at the raw emotions in the depth of his blue eyes. Hope and lust were easy to recognize, but I also saw the same thing I saw every time I looked at myself in a mirror. The fear of being rejected.

Never breaking eye contact, I placed my left hand beside my right. Flattening my palms against his warm skin, I resumed exploring the hard lines of his body.

As my fingers crept lower, I watched in delight as his sky-blue eyes darkened to the blue of the deep sea. His breathing grew rougher, and his muscles flexed under my fingertips.

At any moment, I had expected him to grow impatient, push away my hands, and position himself to enter me. But he didn't.

How was it possible for me to feel more in control while exciting a predator than I'd ever felt while with my matched?

Heart pounding in my ears, I continued moving my hands south until my fingers brushed the base of his erection.

Coda stopped breathing, and his body quivered.

I froze. He'd given me permission to touch him, but had he meant *everywhere*? What if, in my desire to feel wanted and in control, I was taking advantage of him?

Gazing at his face, I searched for any signs of discomfort or annoyance, but found none.

I tentatively brushed my fingers against the base again, thrilling at the full-body shiver it produced in the powerful shifter. "Is it okay if I—"

"Goddess *yesss*." Coda half groaned and half whined. "Please."

I couldn't help my soft laugh at the desperation in his voice. Curling my fingers around his erection, I gently squeezed his thick girth.

"Ellora." He growled my name, sending a shiver down my spine and heat straight between my thighs.

Emboldened by his reactions, I gripped him tighter and ran my hands along his engorged erection. When my fingers teased across the head, Coda's hips involuntarily bucked into my touch.

His eyes closed and his forehead creased. "Sorry. My wolf is making it hard to be still. I want to touch you."

I worked my fingers up and down his velvet length. "Then touch me."

Coda's eyes snapped open, a blue glow encircling the pupil. "Where?"

"Anywhere." The word was off my tongue before I could stop myself.

He moved fast, positioning himself between my legs, but sliding down until his lips kissed me just below my naval. "Does it have to be with my fingers?"

"No," I answered, unsure what else he could mean thanks to the lust fogging my mind and making it hard to concentrate.

Why did I want this man so much? I wasn't in heat, so I couldn't blame my instincts for this. And why did it feel so right? Like I was supposed to be here, with this man?

When his tongue traced the length of my slit, I stopped worrying about why I was drawn to him. Heck, I forgot how to think in complete sentences.

"What... oh!" I squirmed, unsure if I was trying to get away from or get closer to his mouth. "I didn't know it could feel like this."

Coda paused. "You can't mean—"

My cheeks burned as hot as the rest of my body. "Um. My matched weren't in to giving orally. They have busy schedules and said it was a waste of their time."

The wolf shifter between my thighs snarled and his chest vibrated, and for a moment, it was like I was sitting on a speaker that was playing deep bass.

"You aren't saying I'm the first man to eat you... are you, my little dust bunny?" His tongue dipped inside my heat, but his glowing eyes stayed locked on my face.

Between the pet name, his wicked tongue, and Coda calling me his... I forgot to breathe and nearly went cross-eyed with pleasure. "You're the first."

That was the end of Coda's control. His hands gripped my hips, angling me to give him better access. Like a wolf starved, his tongue alternated between delving inside me, and lapping roughly against my clit.

All the while, he rumbled his pleasure as though I was his favorite food. Within seconds, his tongue was reaching deeper and was far rougher than it had been, and I could do little more than choke out strangled sounds of ecstasy as my need for release turned almost painful.

"Come for me, Ellora," Coda commanded.

That was it.

Clamping my legs around his head, I screamed through my release. Coda continued to lick up the wetness between

my thighs greedily as I tried not to pass out from the pleasure short-circuiting my body.

I had no idea how far things would have gone if it
hadn't been for the bedroom door being shoved open.

"CODA! Did you hurt her?" Quin burst into the room,
his chest heaving and eyes flashing. "I heard her scream!"

"I swear, if you brought both a woman and a pet into
this house, I will kill you both—brothers or not!" Macarius
snarled as he stepped into the room behind Quin.

Taking in the scene in front of them, both men froze
mid-step, their mouths agape.

Coda twisted his body around, his muscles flexing as he
prepared to defend me against attack. "Don't insult me,
Quin. I'd never hurt her."

"You brought a rabbit shifter into the house?" Macarius
growled as he realized I was the pet rabbit.

He may have sounded disgusted, but as his eyes trailed
along my exposed skin, I caught the glow of interest in
them. My cheeks burned, and I couldn't decide if I wanted
to cover myself or expose more of myself to his hungry
gaze.

What was wrong with me? Not even five minutes
before, two wolves had been fighting over me, and I'd been
trying to keep from being squished. Then the infamous
Macarius had shown up, and he clearly wasn't happy with
my presence.

Yet rather than fleeing from this house of unstable
predators, I'd let one devour me like I was his own personal
chocolate Easter bunny. Even now, I was more turned on

than I'd ever been in my life, and I wanted to finish what Coda and I had started.

It seemed so wrong to admit that I wanted these men—even the angry, brooding one—who were practically strangers, more than I'd ever craved my matched.

Maybe the separation was affecting me more than I realized, and I was beginning to lose my mind?

Quin shoved past Macarius. Ripping a blanket from the foot of the bed, he bent and tucked it around my body.

"Thank you, Quin." Tears sprung to my eyes at his thoughtfulness.

*Jumpin' jackalope!* I was an emotional mess.

Rather than respond, Quin pressed a kiss to the top of my hair.

Macarius leaned against the doorframe, an unreadable expression on his face. "Gather the female's things. She's not staying here."

Coda leaped to his feet, his hands balling into tight fists at his sides. "Macarius, she needs—"

Macarius curled his lip in disdain. "I don't care what she needs. It isn't my problem."

Rage bubbled in my stomach, but it quickly turned to sadness. He was right. I wasn't their problem... but did he have to be such a jerk about it?

"As I was trying to tell you in the living room, the alpha asked us to—" Quin tried, only to be cut off by Macarius's snort.

"Alpha Cillian knows my stance on sharing my personal space and how I need complete privacy. Take the female back to his home. I'm sure he will find another group of males who will happily take her in."

My stomach quivered, and for the first time since I'd arrived at Monroe's pack, I felt true fear. The thought of being in a house with strange male wolves was terrifying, and my blood turned to ice water in my veins.

In that moment, I realized that while I trusted Monroe, I wouldn't be able to live in a house with wolves. My body would be in a constant state of fight or flight thanks to my inner shifter.

Which made it even stranger that I felt comfortable enough to sleep in between Coda and Quin, and that I was drawn to Macarius, even though he looked ready to snap some necks. Deep in my broken soul, I knew I was safe with them.

"What if we refuse to return her?" Coda crossed his arms over his bare chest and faced off with the larger man.

Quin stepped forward to stand shoulder-to-shoulder with Coda. They'd been ready to kill each other over me, and now they were ready to fight together to keep me. Wolves were complex and confusing creatures.

"Guys…" I tried to speak over the growls rumbling from all three men, but either they couldn't hear me, or I was being ignored.

"Then you will pack your things and be out of this house by the time I return tomorrow evening. I will not sacrifice my solitude just so you two can get laid." Without waiting for a response, Macarius turned on his heel and strode away.

A moment later, the front door slammed with enough force to shake the house's foundation. Just when I was beginning to feel safe, the rug had been ripped from beneath my feet.

Strangely enough, I didn't feel as worried as I probably should have. And I had a sneaking suspicion it had something to do with the glorious backsides of the two naked men in front of me.

## Chapter TEN

### ELLORA

Blowing out a sigh, I stood and tightened the blanket around my body. I squeezed between the brothers and made my way back into the destroyed living room. It took a few minutes, but eventually, I found my backpack beneath an overturned side table.

"What are you doing?" Coda asked.

I turned to find he'd pulled on a pair of loose basketball shorts. It was a shame, but the day had been full of disappointments, so I wasn't surprised. Coda bent and, with a single hand, flipped the oversized couch back into an upright position.

I didn't think I'd ever get used to how freakishly strong wolf shifters were or how physically imposing they were. Then again, maybe they only seemed huge in contrast to my petite form. Rabbit females in general tended to be on the small side, but I'd never given my size much thought until seeing the hulking size of the wolves.

I couldn't help but wonder if they were above average *everywhere*. Of their own accord, my eyes drifted to the waistband of his shorts. Then lower.

The answer to my question was obvious, outlined by the thin material of the shorts. Swallowing hard, I pulled my gaze away and willed myself not to blush.

"Hey. Are you okay?" Quin caught my arm and gently turned me to face him.

I found myself at eye level with his abs. My traitorous tongue slid across my lip, wishing it was his tanned skin.

"I'm, um…" I stammered.

"Of course she isn't," Coda snapped, flopping down on the couch. "We've done a crap job of making her feel safe."

Quin righted an armchair. Sitting down, he pulled me onto his lap.

"That's not true. I do feel safe. Mostly, anyway," I protested. "But I can't say I understand anything that has happened since I woke up."

Quin twisted a lock of my blue hair around his finger. "I'm sorry we scared you this morning. We let our wolves get out of control, and that shouldn't have happened."

I gave him a small smile. "It's okay."

"No, it isn't," Coda mumbled under his breath. "We've never been in this situation before, and we aren't handling it well."

My heart began beating faster, and my fingers curled

tighter in my makeshift blanket-dress. "What situation? Do you mean your wolves acting a little weird with me?"

Maybe they would explain things. Not that it truly mattered, since I was leaving within the hour. That didn't mean I didn't want my curiosity satisfied first, though.

Quin traced my jaw with his finger. "Ellora, our wolves see you as their mate."

"What?" The word came out at a pitch typically reserved for dog whistles.

Both men winced, then chuckled.

"And it isn't just our wolves. We began falling for you the moment we laid eyes on you." Coda gave me a soft smile.

My lungs seized, and I struggled to breathe. "But you can't!"

I would be lying if I said there wasn't a part of me that wanted to shout in joy at their confession, but the logical part of my brain wanted to scream at them to get away from me. My fate was already sealed, and as much as I wished it were different, I knew my story didn't end with a happily ever after.

I'd never heard of a female rabbit claiming new mates after bonding to her matched, so they couldn't claim me as a mate. Could they?

"I think it's a bit too late to convince our wolves." Quin chuckled. "They aren't in the mood for discussing things, which is what caused the squabble earlier."

My eyebrows drew together. "I just don't understand.

Why would I be important enough that your wolves would fight over me?"

Quin caught my face between his rough palms. "Sweet girl, you have no idea how special you are, do you?"

I was too lost in his eyes to form a response.

"Or how much I long to taste your lips and claim you as my mate." Quin's mouth was mere millimeters from my own.

I hadn't heard him move, but Coda's arms wrapped around my middle. "Our wolves fought this morning because they aren't eager to share you, and they are determined to not be outdone by each other."

"B-But Monroe's mates are okay with sharing?" It came out as a question rather than a statement.

"Wolves can successfully share a mate, but it can be challenging in the beginning." Coda pressed kisses to my bare shoulders. "We are competitive beasts who enjoy winning, and we let that cloud our judgment, and it led to the fight."

"My inner shifter already claimed my matched as her mates. I can't undo it." My voice cracked, and my lip quivered.

It was so unfair. If not for my social ladder-climbing parents and the demands of my heat, I would've had a chance at happiness. I could've had mates who loved me.

"Is there a rule that says we can't claim you?" Quin pressed his forehead against mine.

"No. But I don't think I can claim you back. Then you'll

be stuck with a mate who can't complete the bond." My voice cracked, and a tear slid down my cheek.

"What if we're willing to take that risk?" Coda hooked his chin over my shoulder. "Isn't that our choice to make?"

The dam holding back my sorrow broke, and I began to sob.

Sandwiching me between them, the guys stroked my hair and whispered reassurances.

"You don't understand!" I choked out when I finally managed to speak.

Quin used the corner of the blanket to wipe the tears from my face. "What don't we understand, love?"

"You can't love me, because I'm dying." Saying the words out loud was far harder than I'd expected it to be.

Coda gave a low whine, and his arms tightened around my waist.

Quin's face paled. "Dying?"

Dropping my gaze to my lap, I told them the story of being matched, how my parents had betrothed me from the moment I was born, the pain of my first heat, and the way I'd claimed them even though they hadn't reciprocated.

"A rabbit shifter can't be away from her mates for long before it begins to affect her body. Eventually, my body will give out from the stress of separation, or during my next heat—whichever comes first."

The silence stretched out between us as the guys absorbed the news of my impending demise.

"Isn't there anything we could do?" Coda asked, his

breath teasing the hair at the base of my neck and causing me to shiver.

"Not that I know of." Then I admitted in a whisper, "It's already begun."

"Already?" Quin's voice was harsh, but when I glanced up, I found only sorrow etched on his face.

"It's been almost two weeks since I left the burrow. I'm honestly surprised I'm not in worse pain." I picked at a seam on the blanket, not wanting to meet their faces.

Coda pressed his cheek against my back, and the stubble on his jaw tickled my skin. "We will find a way to save you."

Quin placed a gentle kiss on my forehead. "Yes. You just hopped into our lives. It's far too soon for you to leave us."

"Thank you." Closing my eyes, I let myself soak up their attention.

Was this what it was like to be loved?

I tried my best to commit that moment to memory because I knew I wouldn't experience it again.

Through the window, I could see the sun dropping low in the sky. It would be dark soon, so I couldn't leave that night. But at first light, I would be on my way. There was no way I would let my presence split up the three brothers.

Coda sighed. "I need to go update the alpha on Macarius's return." Reluctantly, he released me and stood.

"Ellora, you need to eat. Does anything sound good?" Quin asked.

I found it hard to concentrate on his question, thanks to his hand rubbing my thigh. He meant it as a calming gesture, but the sheer size of his hand meant that his fingers were brushing the sensitive skin high on my thigh.

"Tacos?" My stomach rumbled loudly at the mention of my favorite five-letter word.

The guys laughed, and the tension in the room eased.

"Okay, how about we give you some privacy to clean up or whatever? I'll go talk to the alpha, and Quin can pop down to the taco stand. We can be back in under an hour." Coda held out his hand and pulled me to my feet.

Quin pushed himself out of the seat. "You need to bolt the door behind us, and don't open it for anyone until we return. Got it?"

My stomach wobbled. I was going to be alone.

*Stop being silly, Ellora!* I chided myself. *You need a shower, and there are wolves running security. Besides, no one knows you're here.*

Forcing a smile to my lips, I teased, "I'll be fine! Last I checked, I was a grown adult."

The wolves didn't look entirely comfortable leaving me, but I shooed them out the door before they could change their mind. After clicking the locks into place, I made my way to the bathroom for a much-needed shower.

I SAT ON THE COUCH, staring in horror at the front door.

*BOOM!*

The door shuddered, but the bolts held firm against the assault.

*BOOM!*

Whoever was on the other side of the door, they were determined to get inside.

UGH! Why had I been so stupid in sending Quin to get tacos? Actually, that was a stupid question. I'd asked for tacos because everyone knows that tacos are hugs wrapped in a tortilla. Besides, it was impossible to cry while eating a taco, and I was desperately trying to keep my tears at bay.

The only thing more tragic than dying was dying with an empty stomach.

Low growls came from the other side of the door, letting me know my unwelcome guests were wolves. Could they be from Cillian's pack?

Cillian and Monroe had seemed very confident about my safety. Would their pack mates risk angering the alpha by attacking me?

The wolves continued throwing their bodies against the door, and with each blow, the door creaked louder. It was sturdy, but the wood couldn't hold them off forever. Ignoring my instincts, which were screaming for me to run in the opposite direction, I rushed to the door and pushed a small cabinet in front of it.

Hopefully, that would slow them down long enough for me to figure out what to do. I began to scan the living room, searching for a place to hide. Then, the idiocy of that thought had me rolling my eyes.

Did I seriously think I could beat the paranormal

world's hide-and-go-seek champions? Everyone claims that Sasquatches are the champions, but that's only because the wolf shifters haven't had a desire to sniff them out.

So unless I submerged myself in a tub of perfume or buried myself in a pile of garlic, the wolves would track me with ease. My only hope was to escape out a window or lock myself away until the brothers returned.

Before I could make a move, the door flew open on its hinges and slammed hard against the wall. Two wolves tumbled through the doorway, howling in victory.

Their shaggy red coats were nothing like the sleek carbon coats of Coda and Quin. Saliva dripped from their bared fangs, and their murderous, glowing eyes locked on me.

As the wolves thundered across the wood floor toward me, my instincts kicked in with a vengeance. When they sprung toward me, I dropped to the floor and managed to keep my head attached to my shoulders... barely.

The red wolves skidded to a stop a few feet away and spun around to face me. Their jaws snapped in frustration at being thwarted.

"Back down! You're supposed to help us get her, not kill her!" a familiar voice shouted to be heard over the snarls and growls coming from the pair of wolves.

*Brett.*

My heart plummeted to the center of the earth.

They'd found me.

Inch-by-inch, I began moving away from the wolves and toward the hallway. I knew if I moved too fast, I'd excite their animalistic instincts, and the hunt would be on. There wasn't a chance the wolves would be stopped before they managed to rip out my throat.

Three men stepped through the doorway behind Brett.

All four of my matched were here.

"Ellora. You should have known better than to run," Henry scolded, clicking his tongue against his teeth in a mocking *tsk-tsk* sound.

"In the history of our burrow, there hasn't been a female who shamed herself by running from her matched... until you." Edward's skin was turning an angry, mottled red. "Rumors spread fast through the burrows, and you've embarrassed us in front of our peers."

Edward ran his fingers through his perfectly trimmed hair. "Hades, Ellora! My boss stopped by my office to offer his sympathy! We've been forced to lie through our teeth, but we've finally convinced almost everyone you were out of town visiting a sick friend, and we were coming to support you through it."

If they were waiting for me to speak, they were going to be waiting until hell started serving perfectly chilled iced caramel macchiato.

Even if I could have spoken past the lump of fear and anxiety stuck in my throat, I had nothing to say to them. Ever.

"Let's grab her and get out of here before the wolves return." Jay shoved forward, and I realized it was now or never.

Harnessing the adrenaline coursing through my veins, I

scrambled to my feet and tore off down the hallway. The sound of the wolves' claws scratching the wooden floor came from behind me, and it was only a matter of seconds before they were snapping at my legs.

Sharp teeth sank into my calf, sending pain exploding up my leg before he lost his hold on my skin and his teeth ripped free. Biting back my shriek of pain, I threw myself into the first open doorway and slammed the door before the wolves could get a second bite.

Locking the door, I frantically searched the bathroom for something I could push in front of it. I knew I couldn't stop my attackers, but maybe I could slow them down.

Sadly, the modern minimalist decor made that impossible. The only cabinet in the room was beneath the sink and screwed to the wall.

The door shuddered as the wolves threw their bodies against it, reminding me it was only a matter of time before I had company.

"ELLORA!" Brett roared my name. "STOP THIS NONSENSE! Like it or not, you're going home with us."

The heck I was. "You should leave before I cut off your ball sack and wear it as a swim cap!"

I didn't know how this fiasco was going to end, but I knew it wasn't with me being dragged back to the burrows. If I could hold them off long enough, maybe Coda and Quin would walk in and stop this madness.

Rushing across the expansive bathroom, I skidded across the marble floor and slid into the glass shower. It was larger than my closet back at the burrows.

I bet it was big enough to fit me and all three wolves at the same time...

What was wrong with me? I was in the middle of a life-and-death crisis, but rather than freaking out, I was daydreaming about shower sex with the wolves who'd taken me in.

It was nothing more than a dream anyway, since Macarius seemed like he'd prefer to stare into the sun than look at me. I could already imagine him walking in and cursing at the bloody mess my dead body made in his pristine white bathroom.

Standing on tiptoe, I ran my fingers around the frame of the large frosted window, searching for a latch or a way to open it. Nada.

Rushing to the toilet, I snatched up the metal toilet paper stand. I hurried back to the window and steadied my trembling limbs.

Taking up a baseball batter's stance, I gathered my strength and swung with my entire body. The metal crashed against the glass with bone-jarring force, but the glass was so thick that it didn't even chip, let alone shatter like I'd hoped.

Either I was weak as a newborn kitten, or these wolves had installed bulletproof glass in their bathroom. Who even did that?

*CRACK!*

I twisted my neck to find the wooden door beginning to splinter under the red wolves' violent battering. Thank fluff the narrow hallway had kept them from backing up and throwing their full strength against the door.

Still, I knew my time was up.

If I couldn't take on a window and win, there wasn't a chance I'd win against the mangy wolves and four men.

While I didn't think the rabbit shifters would physically harm me, I found I preferred taking my chances with the rabid-looking wolves.

With that thought burning my mind, I closed my eyes and allowed my shift to ripple down my body. When it was over, I was left in my most vulnerable form.

I lay quivering and partially hidden beneath my favorite worn shirt I'd slipped into after Coda had left. It didn't take psychic abilities to know what was going to happen when the door caved in.

Any second, the wolves would rush into the bathroom. They'd easily get to me before any of the rabbit shifter men could, and with their instincts stirred into a frenzy, the wolves would sink their sharp canines into my tiny bunny body without hesitation.

It was a tale as old as time and a natural part of the circle of life.

The upside was that my death at the hands of the wolves would be instantaneous. Plus, my matched would get a front-row seat to see the wolves fight over my bunny body as they ripped me in two like a wishbone on Thanksgiving.

A malicious satisfaction settled over me. My parting gift

to my ex-mates would be a lifetime of nightmares and therapy.

The bathroom door imploded under the wolves' strength, shaking the house as the pieces crashed into the floor. Without slowing, the pair of red wolves surged toward me, their paws thundering against the marble floor.

Time seemed to slow as I watched the scene play out in front of me. The wolves lunged toward me, bits of drool flying around them.

Behind them, the four rabbit shifter men shoved their way into the room. Their faces contorted into masks of horror and anger as they realized the weak point in their plan.

They couldn't stop the wolves—at least not in time to prevent my death. If I'd been in human form, I would have thrown up the loser sign just to rub a little salt in the wound.

I didn't want to die, but I was going to go out knowing they'd lost too. A few seconds of physical pain was far better than a lifetime of letting them kill off my soul a little each day.

*Five...*

*Four...*

The wolves' muscles flexed, and they leaped toward me, jaws open and their razor-sharp fangs glistening with saliva.

*Three...*

*Tw—*

I didn't make it to one.

Instead, an earthquake shook the house, and the glass of the window above my head shattered.

For a moment, I felt as though I were caught in a snow globe, except instead of snow, shards of glass fell around me like a million glittering diamond raindrops. It was beautiful, and such a stark contrast to the hellhound-like beast that landed in front of me with a deafening howl.

# Chapter ELEVEN

## MACARIUS

Pulling into the abandoned parking lot of a long-closed store, I put my car into park.

"What were they thinking?" I snarled, slamming my hand against the steering wheel.

My brothers knew my boundaries when it came to bringing outsiders into our home. Reese enjoyed pushing boundaries, but since she'd moved out and was no longer sneaking friends in, the only person who'd stepped foot inside our house was Cillian.

I couldn't be too mad at my brothers. They'd believed I wouldn't return this soon, but that knowledge did little to calm my inner turmoil.

At that moment, I doubted anything could quiet the building storm inside me when her intoxicating fragrance still filled my lungs, and the sight of her bare skin was burned on my retinas.

My wolf had never been a stable beast, and I'd long ago learned that the best way to remain in control was to limit the amount of time I spent with people outside my family. That allowed my wolf to decompress before being forced out into public again.

It was a precarious balance, but thus far, my rigid boundaries had kept me from killing anyone who didn't deserve it.

I'd been forced to return from my trip early because, although I'd rented a house far from the city that would give me a place to retreat to each evening, my wolf had remained on edge.

Unable to trust him not to go off during one of the meetings, I'd decided to return home for a couple days to give him time in familiar settings to find his inner peace. At the very least, I hoped he'd find a scrap of patience and not want to rip people's throats out for simply breathing too loud or asking idiotic questions.

Unfortunately, when I'd walked into the house to find my brothers battling for dominance and trying to force each other to submit, it had ramped up my wolf's agitation.

I still could have held it together if it hadn't been for the sweet scent that slapped me in the face.

*Her* scent.

I couldn't understand how the way she smelled affected me like that, especially when I'd yet to catch sight of any female in the house.

My wolf proved to be quicker than me on the uptake

and had put the pieces together. The mystery female was my mate.

And that meant Coda and Quin were fighting over what was mine.

I'd remained in control of my wolf by the skin of my teeth. There was no doubt in my mind that if I'd shifted, their battle for dominance would have become a fight to the death.

Their death. Not mine.

Coda had grabbed a black ball of fur from the floor and retreated down the hall.

Ignoring him, I'd searched the room for the source of the delicate fragrance, all the while ignoring the excuses Quin was spouting for why they'd brought a pet into the house. If I hadn't been struggling with controlling my wolf, I would have realized the rabbit was a shifter.

At the feminine scream coming from Coda's room, Quin had forgotten all about me and rushed down the hallway like a man possessed. I'd followed, and when he flung open the bedroom door, her scent enveloped us.

My eyes dropped to the woman, who was partially hidden by Coda's body. Her face was flushed, and her mouth was parted as she tried to steady her breathing. Coda's self-satisfied face as he ran his tongue across his bottom lip and the sweet scent of her arousal told me the woman's cry hadn't been one of pain.

Other than Monroe, the blue-haired beauty was the smallest female I'd ever seen. Hades, compared to my size, she might as well have been a sprite or a fairy.

That was when the final piece of the puzzle fell into place.

The rabbit my brothers had brought home was a shifter, and she was my mate. Pain tore at my insides as I realized I could never have her.

Fate had dealt me a wolf who was a mere breath away from turning feral. Now, in some twisted joke, she'd decided to give me the most fragile of shifters as a mate.

I wanted nothing more than to scoop the tiny female off the floor and swear my undying devotion while worshipping her body. But I could never trust myself, or my wolf, around her.

The only way to keep her safe was to get her as far away from me as possible.

Dropping my head back against the seat, I closed my eyes and tried to ignore my wolf's heartbroken howl as it echoed around my skull. He was desperate to return to her, but as much as I longed for the same, I couldn't allow it.

*MINE.*

My eyes flew open. I'd heard of wolves speaking, but mine had seemed too animalistic to understand words. This was the first time he'd chosen to communicate using human language.

*Protect. Mine,* he urged, pacing anxiously.

"I am protecting her—by keeping her away from us," I whispered into the quiet of the car.

*NO!* My wolf rammed against the invisible barriers I used to keep him under control. *We protect.*

"Sit down and act like a good dog," I snapped, sick of

being forced to keep my inner beast muzzled and on a leash to prevent him from going on a killing spree. "Maybe if she'd been a female wolf, I could trust you not to kill her if my control slipped. But she's too small, and even a tiny mistake could end up with her being injured."

*Never.* My wolf grew still, no longer fighting for control. *Never hurt.*

Pressing my fingers to my eyes, I groaned in frustration. I longed to believe him, but the past had taught me that my wolf's instincts were far stronger than his intentions.

My wolf wasn't ready to give up. *Please.* Dropping to his stomach, he released a pitiful whine.

My resolve crumbled under his puppy eyes and my own need to be close to her. "We'll go back and sit outside the house to keep watch, but we're not going in."

Compromise reached, I put the car into gear and headed back to the house.

PULLING my car under the cover of some overhanging branches, I flicked off my headlights. I was far enough away that Coda and Quin were unlikely to sense my presence.

Even at this distance, my sharp vision allowed me to see four unfamiliar men pushing their way inside the house.

Without making a sound, I stepped from my car and listened to the voices.

*Protect. Protect. Protect.* My wolf's demand pounded like the beat of a drum in my head.

*Be calm. I'm trying to discern why they're here.* I refused to rush in just because he didn't want any other males near her.

Not that I blamed him. Every time the image of Coda on top of her as they kissed popped into my mind, my blood pressure rose.

But if I wanted to avoid a bloodbath, I needed to stay away from her. I had ordered Coda and Quin to remove her, so maybe the men were there to escort her to a new house.

A house where she would be safe from me.

Unable to help myself, I began moving through the trees that surrounded the house. I removed my suit jacket and shirt as I stalked closer and tossed them carelessly over a low-hanging tree branch.

If she needed me, I was prepared to shift.

My ears strained to hear the sound of her voice. If these men had been invited by my brothers or sent by my alpha, I didn't want to reveal my presence.

I knew my wolf; he would likely rip someone's throat out just to avoid small talk. And I was in a foul enough mood to let him.

A new thought caused my stomach to twist. I'd refused to listen to their reasons for bringing her into our home. What if she was in danger from someone or something outside the pack?

No, Coda and Quin wouldn't have left her side if that were true. Besides, how much trouble could one tiny female get into? What reason would someone have to hunt her down?

My answer came when one of the men yelled.

"ELLORA! STOP THIS NONSENSE! Like it or not, you're going home with us."

He couldn't have been more wrong.

For the first time in my life, I released my wolf from every barrier and gave him full control. They had threatened our girl—Ellora, he had called her—and now I was going to send them to hell to face judgment for it.

I took off at a run, shifting smoothly from human to wolf without slowing my pace. Once all four of my heavy paws landed on the spongy earth, my speed increased until I moved across the ground like a blurred shadow.

It was a pace no wolf on earth could keep up with.

Not even the alpha.

"You should leave before I cut off your ball sack and wear it as a swim cap!"

I stumbled slightly in shock at the melodic voice of our mate handing out threats like it was her side hustle.

*Violent.* My wolf huffed in amusement. *Sexy.*

With those words, she'd stolen my wolf's heart completely. I just hoped she was ready for what that would mean. And I hoped he'd keep his word to never hurt her.

As I neared the house, I could hear the creak of the hinges and the harsh pants of the wolves as they savagely threw themselves against a door. I hadn't seen the wolves enter, but now that I was close, I could smell the sour scent that identified them as rogues.

Straining my ears, I picked out seven unique heartbeats. Four men, two wolves, and Ellora. Her heart was galloping at a worrisome speed. She was scared.

*Protect.* My wolf bared his fangs and lurched forward, moving faster and faster with each stride. *Kill.*

I'd reached the edge of the yard when the sound of the bathroom door splintering under the weight of the wolves came from the house.

Time was up.

Tuned into the rhythm of her racing heart, I heard the moment it slowed. And knowing why she'd grown calm hit me like a sword through the stomach.

Ellora was facing death and had accepted her fate.

But she'd miscalculated, because I knew with certainty I would never let her leave me. And while I didn't have a clue how she'd ended up in this mess, I was ready and willing to clean it up.

*Agreed.*

It had taken years, but my wolf and I were truly one for the first time in my life. And we'd never been more powerful.

This is why I didn't bother running to the front door and headed straight for the large bathroom window. Without hesitation, I dug my claws into the soft earth and launched my massive wolf body straight at the window.

I'd paid a ridiculous amount of money for the unbreakable glass panes, but if I hadn't known better, I would have guessed the window was little more than a thin piece of ice.

I'd already taken in the scene before my paws hit the bathroom floor. My eyes followed the trail of honeysuckle-scented blood smeared across the floor to where it ended in the shower. A tiny bunny with fur the color of my soul lay partially hidden beneath a piece of fabric.

Anger had been something I'd experienced on a near-daily basis for my entire adult life. But that anger was nothing compared to the all-consuming rage that pumped through my veins at the sight of her blood.

They'd hurt my mate.

I locked eyes with the two wolves barreling toward her. Realizing they'd need to get through me first, they tried to stop their forward motion, but they couldn't gain traction on the floor.

Even if they could have stopped themselves, it wouldn't have mattered. I had already decided they weren't leaving that bathroom alive.

Calling on our speed, I blurred toward the wild-eyed wolf that had smears of crimson blood on his muzzle.

My mate's blood.

Sinking my fangs into his neck, I flipped him over with a violent speed that caused his neck to snap. He hadn't even had the chance to make a sound before his life was snuffed out.

The instant the wolf went limp in my hold, I dropped him and twisted around to catch the second wolf in my powerful jaws. This wolf was larger than the first, but he was only half my size. It wasn't a fair fight, but he hadn't cared about fairness when he'd wanted to devour my mate.

With the back of the wolf's neck between my jaws, I shook him by his scruff like he was nothing more than a stuffed toy. I let him experience the pain of what it was like to be prey caught in a larger predator's mouth—which was exactly what he would've done to Ellora if I hadn't been here.

His death came far quicker than I would have liked, but it was just as well, because the four men had roused from their shocked stupor and were scrambling toward the front door.

My wolf longed to kill them with the same efficiency as he'd dispatched the rogues. But I wanted answers first.

I barreled through the open doorway and into the narrow hall. Without hesitation, I leaped onto the first man's back and rode his body to the floor, taking one of the other men down with us.

The man beneath me slammed his head against the hardwood and went limp.

Hopefully, he wasn't dead.

Tilting my head, I studied the motionless body. There was a faint heartbeat, so he might make it. Besides, there were three more I could get answers from.

Baring my teeth, I herded them into a corner of the living room. Once they were pinned, I shifted back to my human form and stalked toward them.

"I'm going to handcuff you. My wolf longs for your death, so if you fight me, I will kill you and enjoy it."

Reaching into one of the TV stand drawers, I pulled out several pairs of handcuffs and chains.

I liked being prepared.

"You can't do this! It goes against the shifter code!" one of the men spat.

Interesting. They were shifters? I'd been so focused on the rogue wolves and my beautiful Ellora, I hadn't paid much attention to the men. Even if they'd been armed with a gun, they posed little threat to me.

Pausing, I drew their scent deep into my lungs, and a slow smile spread across my lips. They were rabbit shifters.

*Delicious.* My wolf practically drooled at the possibility of a hunt.

A twinge of worry shot through my chest. What if he forgot Ellora was our mate? Was the pull of the mate bond stronger than the drive to hunt?

Only time would tell.

It was too late to backtrack now. She was mine, and we'd find a way to make this work.

I yanked the man's arms behind his back far harder than necessary.

"We were only taking back our property! You have no right to bar us from Ellora," he protested, his eyes blazing with righteous indignation.

"There is nothing in this house that belongs to you," I grunted, kicking aside the rug that covered the metal loops bolted to the floor along the wall.

I used a chain to connect each pair of handcuffs to one of

the metal rings. It took less than a minute to get all four men handcuffed and chained to the floor.

The cuffs were laced with magic that prevented the men from shifting forms. They weren't leaving until I said they could.

*If* I said they could.

"She's our mate!" a second man yelled. "We have the papers showing she belongs to us—" The man fell silent—probably due to the fist I slammed into his face.

His eyes rolled back, and he slumped against the wall. Growing impatient with the need to check on Ellora, I decided this was taking too long.

The two conscious men stared up at me in wide-eyed horror as I grabbed a fistful of their hair and cracked their skulls together. I was careful to only cause enough damage to keep their shifter magic busy healing them, but not enough to cause permanent injury.

Satisfied they were all out cold and chained up snug as bugs on my rug, I headed back down the hallway.

As I drew closer to the bathroom, my bloodlust morphed into something else. Something that was gentler and far darker at the same time.

I wanted to claim her soul and corrupt her body, but I also wanted to cradle her in my arms as she slept, making sure she knew that no one would dare to hurt her again.

Not wanting to alarm her more than necessary, I grabbed a pair of slacks from my room and put them on before heading into the bathroom. Stepping into the room, I saw Ellora had scooted beneath the shirt, completely covering her face.

I grimaced as I looked at the two dead wolves sprawled on the floor, their necks twisted at unnatural angles. The rogues were surrounded by what remained of the door and millions of glass shards.

All the pieces came together to paint a savage scene. It wasn't surprising she'd hidden her face from it.

Making my way to her side, I began to worry she might be more seriously injured than I'd suspected. Lifting the shirt, I peered down at the ball of black fur.

Bright blue eyes blinked up at me.

Slowly, so as not to frighten her, I gently began to check her body for injuries. When I found the bite on her leg, I cast a look at the rogue and wished I could raise him from the dead so I could kill him again.

Her injury wasn't serious, and thanks to her shifter side, the wound had nearly stopped bleeding, but I still wanted to clean and bandage it.

Before I could stop myself, I'd swept her up into my arms, needing to reassure my wolf and myself that she was safe.

I'd expected Ellora to panic at being held by a stranger who'd demanded she leave his house not too long ago. But she only stiffened for a moment before her muscles relaxed, and she sagged against my chest.

I decided then and there that I was never going to put her down.*Never,* my wolf rumbled in agreement.

# Chapter TWELVE

## QUIN

I raced up the driveway to the house. Coda was just ahead of me. He was moving as fast as he could without dropping any of the bags of food he was balancing.

Slowing my pace, I reached out and grabbed the bag that teetered precariously on top. "Did you get a text too?"

"Yeah. But why would Macarius text us to come back to the house?"

I didn't respond because I didn't have an answer. As we drew closer to the door, the scent of rogues caused the hair on my body to rise.

What if the rogues had hurt Ellora? Why had we been so stupid and left her alone? Would I find her missing—or worse, dead—when I opened the door?

With a shaking hand, I twisted the dented brass knob.

The door groaned as it swung open on a single undamaged hinge to reveal a sight my brain couldn't begin to process.

Macarius sat in his favorite black leather armchair. His chest was bare, and he wore nothing but a pair of his perfectly tailored slacks.

He was studying the four men chained to our floor with a stormy expression I was all too familiar with and knew it promised violence was on the horizon.

Finding four strangers chained to the floor in front of my older brother wasn't the weird part, though. No, the most shocking part of the scene was the black ball of fur stretched out on his thigh as though she were a lap cat instead of a bunny.

Her eyelids fluttered as Macarius's fingers gently stroked along her ears and down her back. He was petting her of his own free will.

What in Dante's hell had happened while we were gone?

"Did I walk into an alternate reality?" Coda murmured under his breath.

I sucked in a steadying breath, only to have the scent of blood fill my lungs and clear the confusion clouding my mind.

Dropping the bag of food to the floor, I rushed toward Ellora. "Is she hurt?"

Macarius released a growl that shouldn't have been possible in his human form.

He curled his hand around Ellora protectively, and his massive palm nearly covered her completely. "Back off."

Meeting Macarius's eyes, I was shocked to find a very real threat there, and a trickle of unease slid down my spine.

I'd grown up knowing he was always in my corner, ready to defend his family with ruthless efficiency. But looking into his eyes, I understood that if it came down to it, he would protect Ellora first.

"Mac?" There was no hiding the disbelief in my voice.

"There are two rogues in the bathroom. Take care of their bodies," Macarius ordered.

Standing tall, I set my jaw. "I'm not leaving this room until I know what's going on."

He might be the oldest sibling, but I did not bow to him. I didn't know what had caused the sudden change in his stance when it came to Ellora, but if he thought he could take her from me, he would have a fight on his hands.

Macarius held my gaze for far longer than was comfortable, but I refused to look away. "We'll discuss this later."

Satisfied that he knew it wasn't over, I moved to stand beside his chair. Crossing my arms over my chest, I glared at the four men on the floor.

Coda placed the food bags in the kitchen and took up a position on the opposite side of the armchair. The four men appeared to be uneasy rather than terrified. So they were either brave or stupid.

"We want to speak with your alpha," one of the men demanded.

"Oh, you will. But not until I get answers." Macarius's voice was cold as ice. "Names."

One by one, the guys gave their names. They included their job titles, proving they were the pretentious pricks I'd pegged them to be.

"Why are you in our house?" Coda barked, rocking on the balls of his feet as though readying to attack.

Macarius shot him a look, but Coda ignored him. We might be his younger brothers, but tonight, Macarius would discover we weren't going to be pushed around when it came to Ellora and her safety.

"We weren't going to take anything other than what belongs to us." The guy called Edward leveled a haughty look at us.

It would have been more impressive if not for the ugly purplish bruise circling his eye. Macarius had let off some steam before we arrived.

"Ellora doesn't belong to you." Macarius's voice was flat, as though he were uninterested. I'd learned long ago it was a warning sign that he was at his most volatile.

Jay was the next to speak. "I think there is a misunderstanding since burrows run differently from packs."

"We are aware. In our experience, burrows are far more backward than packs." My words dripped with disgust. I'd seen how Monroe was treated, and it had caused me to lose all respect for rabbit shifters.

Jay's mask of sincerity dropped, and he leaned forward, pulling on his chains. "Big words coming from flea-bitten dogs."

The insult was uncreative and didn't warrant a reaction from my brothers or myself.

Ellora didn't agree. She grunted and pinned her ears against her body.

"Don't stress, my darling," Macarius purred.

My jaw went slack, and I jerked my head in his direction so fast my neck popped. Since when did the big bad wolf learn how to sound anything other than gruff?

And why was he calling Ellora his darling when he'd told us to kick her out just over an hour before?

Brett snorted. "Darling? Yours? According to our trackers, she has been here less than three days." He eyed Ellora. "Don't tell me you've found a way to bring more shame onto yourself! It wasn't enough to embarrass your parents, us, and yourself by abandoning the fate you were assigned? How do you think the burrow will feel when they find out you were willing to whore yourself to the wolves for protection?"

When Ellora had told us her story, she'd glossed over the part about her mates being total douche canoes. She'd given us the impression they were too busy with work to bother bonding with her.

A far different picture was beginning to take shape. Raw fury clogged my throat, making it impossible for me to breathe, let alone speak.

Coda covered the distance between us, and the rabbit shifters faster than my eyes could track. His fist connected with Brett's face with a satisfying crack. "Watch your mouth."

Brett spat blood on the floor, then grinned up at Coda. "I'm only speaking the truth. What I don't understand is why she'd give up living like a princess on our estate for"—his eyes roamed around the room, assessing it—"this."

Our home wasn't a showy mansion, but by no means was it small. Macarius had designed it with a focus on providing for our needs rather than flaunting our wealth—which would have been a waste anyway, since we didn't exactly have visitors.

Seeing the rabbit turn his nose up at a home that cost well into the seven digits to build let me know we were dealing with old-money snobs who believed their wealth, rather than their character, entitled them to respect. They were going to be ticked off when they realized we weren't intimidated by the number of zeros in their bank account.

"So if it isn't the house or money, what could you possibly be providing her that would keep her here?" Jay curled his lip at me as though I were nothing more than gum on the bottom of his shoe.

"Cuddles, snuggles, and so much dick!"

At the sound of her feminine voice, seven sets of eyes focused on Ellora.

She'd shifted to her human form and held a decorative pillow against her middle. It was large enough to cover her—mostly.

"Dick?" Coda and I croaked out at the same time.

If she meant we'd acted like dicks by fighting over her, destroying the house, nearly trampling her, and Macarius demanding she leave, then yeah, she'd probably had her fill of dicks. But as much as I wish it were different, I'd yet to experience the bliss of making love to her.

Henry's skin had taken on a green hue, as though he were moments away from vomiting. The other three appeared to be having problems with their blood pressure.

Ellora stared them down, not realizing she looked ridiculously tiny, sitting astride one of Macarius's thickly muscled thighs.

One glance at Macarius's face told me the rest of the room had ceased to exist. His eyes were glowing as they traveled down her bare back.

Macarius leaned forward, and I wasn't surprised when he curled his fingers around her hips—because it is exactly what I would have done if she'd been sitting naked on my leg.

The Ellora we'd brought home had been scared, exhausted, and little more than a shadow of this bold beauty sitting confidently in Macarius's lap.

"Ellora! Please tell us you haven't let these beasts drool on your skin and paw at you." The muscles in Henry's jaw flexed.

Ellora's anger brought color to her pale cheeks, and with her blue hair falling wildly around her face, she looked like an avenging goddess.

None of us could have anticipated what was about to happen.

Without breaking eye contact with Henry, Ellora lifted her arm and reached behind her. She ran her fingers through Macarius's short beard before moving her hand to cradle the back of his head.

"It just so happens I love their doggy slobber." Her defiance was adorable as she guided Mac to her neck.

My brother didn't need to be asked twice. Leaning forward, he pressed his lips to her skin.

Macarius's chest vibrated with a guttural moan, and his arm snaked around her middle. He slid her up his thigh until her back was pressed against his chest.

All the while, he continued to kiss and lap at the delicate skin of her neck, having forgotten that anyone else existed other than the rabbit shifter on his lap.

"Oh!" Ellora's eyes widened with surprise, then darkened with desire. "Ooooh…"

"Tell the animal to get his mouth off you before he starts humping you like the wild beast he is." Brett yanked hard against his restraints. "Your body is for our pleasure, and you're letting him taint it."

"Ellora! Are you listening?" Jay snarled. "You will obey us! Come here now!"

For the first time since Ellora had shifted to her human form, Macarius's eyes focused on the four men struggling to free themselves.

"Ellora isn't a pet to be ordered around and amuse you," Macarius said between placing hungry kisses along her bare shoulder.

"You know nothing about our ways!" Henry shrieked, his skin becoming mottled with barely contained rage. "She belongs to us, and we have the papers to prove it!"

"Wrong. Ellora can do whatever she pleases." Macarius's voice held a note that had me glancing at Coda in concern.

"And where do you get off thinking you have any right to weigh in on a personal matter?" Brett had managed to get to his knees, and the veins in his neck bulged as he strained against the chains.

These men weren't used to being told no, and it showed.

"Because Ellora is mine, and she has the bite to prove it." I watched in shock as Macarius sank his sharp canines into the tender flesh of Ellora's neck.

By marking her, Ellora had become a wolf's mate, and wolves believed mates were priceless treasures rather than property.

The rabbit shifters might have the power that comes with money and status, but Ellora had a pack of wolves ready to protect her if these men dared to touch a single hair on her head.

"Call the alpha and have him take custody of these men until their burrow can be contacted." Macarius's voice was rough, making the words hard to understand.

Not waiting for a response, he used his unnatural speed to blur from the room, taking Ellora with him.

The living room descended into chaos, with the clattering of chains and the rabbits' shouted threats... but it barely registered.

All I could think about was how Macarius had marked my mate.

I was going to kill him.

# Chapter THIRTEEN

## ELLORA

**M**acarius spun me in his arms so I faced him and my mouth was at the same height as his. With our size difference, this meant my legs were wrapped around him mid-chest rather than around his waist like a normal couple.

But we weren't a normal couple. Not by any stretch of the imagination.

I was at the bottom of the shifter food chain, while he'd looked like a wolf from the depths of hell as he ripped into the rogue wolves. When I'd wanted to defend the wolves from my fluffle's cruel insults, I'd encouraged Macarius to touch me, to kiss me.

Although he'd acted completely different from the man who'd demanded I leave his house, I hadn't been sure he'd even want that level of intimacy with me. Oh, how wrong I'd been.

Not only had he accepted my invitation, but to my utter shock, Macarius had buried his teeth into my neck. He'd shamelessly marked me right there in front of the four rabbit shifters and his brothers.

There was no denying I'd been drawn to him, even when he was acting like a tyrant and bossing everyone around. When he'd come to my rescue, my heart had latched onto him more. I'd hidden under my shirt, listening as he took down the rabbit shifters, but too afraid to come out.

Not for fear of dying—I'd come to terms with that. But for fear I'd embarrass myself by throwing myself at him. I wanted him, just as much as I wanted Coda and Quin.

When Macarius had returned to the bathroom and lifted me into his arms, I'd been unnerved at the powerful pull I felt toward him. My second surprise came as my body relaxed, and my discomfort was muffled.

With each passing hour, the pain from the separation was becoming harder to ignore. Shortly after Coda and Quin had left me alone in the house, every cell in my body had started to burn in agony. It had continued to get worse until I found myself curled on the couch, struggling against alternating urges to vomit and pass out.

The pain had intensified when the rabbit shifters entered the bathroom, which was probably my animal instincts trying to force me back into the arms of my matched. No matter how bad things got, I would never degrade myself by allowing those men to touch me again.

I'd expected my rabbit to fight me to get to her mates,

but she'd remained quiet, curled into a ball in my mind. Instincts should have driven her crazy with the need for her claimed mates' touch, but she acted as though they didn't exist.

How was it possible that the bond I'd formed to my fluffle had snapped, but yet I was still experiencing the repercussions of being separated from them?

I wished I could speak to the elders, but I knew they wouldn't ever give a disgraced bunny their valuable time. They would likely lock me away from the rest of the burrow if I so much as showed my face there again.

Despite how unlikely it seemed, I was beginning to suspect the wolves were easing my pain, but at the same time, they were stirring emotions I didn't expect to experience in this lifetime.

Macarius slammed the door behind us and followed up by locking it with an ancient-looking set of bolts. No one was getting in or out of the room unless he wanted it.

My heart tripped over its rhythm, and my insides twisted. I was trapped in the room with the most terrifying man I'd ever met.

A man who'd just staked his claim on me.

His mouth traveled from my lips and down my neck, distracting me from the precarious situation I was in. I ran my fingers through his dark hair, loving the rumbles of pleasure coming from his chest.

When Macarius sucked my nipple into the heat of his mouth, I couldn't stifle my moan. Heat rushed between my thighs, causing me to become slick with need.

I was quickly reminded that I was nude, and my core was pressed against his bare chest. Which meant his chest was likely becoming wet with the evidence of my desire. My cheeks burned with a mixture of embarrassment and no small amount of lust.

I tried to squirm free from his hold, but Macarius wasn't about to allow it. "Why are you trying to get away from me, little one?" His husky whisper had another wave of slick need rushing between my thighs.

Again, I tried to move my legs so that I could close them, and Macarius responded by pressing my back against the wall. His teeth nipped my neck. "Answer me."

How could I voice what was embarrassing me without causing myself to die of even more embarrassment?

Macarius hesitated and pulled his head back to meet my eyes. "Do you not want this? I'm sorry if I misunderstood, Ellora. I'm doing my best to go slow, but my wolf isn't making it easy. If you don't want this, say the word."

"No! I want you too much!" I blurted out, wanting to ease the worry from his gorgeous face.

Macarius lifted a brow, unconvinced.

Dropping my eyes from his face, I mumbled, "You're making me wet, and I didn't want to make your chest dirty."

"Look at me." Macarius's purr was nearly my undoing.

Still, I couldn't meet his eyes.

Macarius gripped my hips, holding me still against the wall as he ground his chest against me. My legs quivered as electric shocks of pleasure sizzled through me.

"Look at me," he repeated.

I wasn't a virgin, and I'd had plenty of sex during my heat. But it had been straight to the point, slit-and-slam style. This was far more intimate.

Macarius tightened his grip on my hips and began grinding my aching core against his chest. He didn't stop until my breathing was coming in short gasps.

"Look at me." He growled the order, and this time, I lifted my chin to meet his glowing brown eyes. "That's a good girl."

My body trembled, and I nearly came undone at those words.

"Never feel bad about your body's reactions. It is natural and beautiful." Macarius's finger brushed against my core, sending a jolt through my body. He slid his finger along my slit and then lifted the finger to his mouth. "And just as delicious as I knew you would be."

My body burned hotter as I watched his tongue lick my wetness from his finger. When he finished, his hand moved back to my hip.

"Now put your arms around my neck, keep your eyes on mine, and use me." Macarius's orders were doing crazy things to my body.

And in a lust-filled daze, I obeyed him. Wrapping my arms around his neck, I used his shoulders to lift myself slightly so I could find the friction I craved.

The hardest part was keeping my eyes on his face, but I couldn't deny having him watch me as I pleasured myself was wildly erotic. My body was too sensitive and far too worked up to last long.

"Macarius!" I hissed his name, and my back arched as pleasure exploded through me.

"So beautiful," he growled, holding me tight between him and the wall as I twitched with orgasmic aftershocks. His lips found my skin, tasting and sucking up the column of my neck. "Mine."

That single word pulled me from the fog of bliss.

"Macarius?" I caught his face between my palms. "I'm so sorry!"

Confused, he lifted a single eyebrow. "You have nothing to be sorry for."

"Because I've made a mess of everything! I was furious listening to my matched throwing insults at you, Coda, and Quin. All I could think about was proving how wrong they were and making them angry." I hesitated, then confessed, "That isn't the whole truth."

"Color me intrigued." Macarius wrapped his arms around me and moved to sit on the large bed. "Let's hear it, my love."

He kept saying I belonged to him, but as much as I wanted that to be true, I feared I'd trapped him in a one-sided bond.

Taking a deep breath, I bared my soul. "The truth is, being on your lap—petted and protected—it was a turn-on. Seeing my fluffle lose their crap when they realized I wasn't under their control was thrilling. They made me feel worthless, as though they were doing me a favor when they gave me a few minutes of their time."

Macarius's jaw clenched, and his eyes narrowed.

Worried I would lose my nerve, I rushed to finish what I needed to say before he tossed me out on my bum for trapping him. "Macarius, I was already desperate to feel your touch on my human skin. Then I got caught up in the moment, and I wanted them to feel powerless as they watched you kiss me—as they watched someone else touch what they would never have again. It was unfair of me to use you like that."

Macarius twisted around, dropping my back on the pale blue linen bedspread and pinning me beneath his huge, tanned body. "You didn't use me. But here's what you need to understand, darling. I want you to use me. I want you to take whatever you want or need from me. I'm yours."

Tears filled my eyes, blurring my vision. "But what if I can't claim you and complete the bond? I was matched with Brett, Henry, Jay, and Edward. It was an arranged mating that had nothing to do with love. My heat came before I could run. When I was at my most vulnerable, my parents handed me off to my matched. I tried to resist, but I'd been in agony, and the heat stirred my instincts to mate into a frenzy. In an effort to escape the pain and lost to the heat, I accepted their bodies." Not wanting to see the disgust on his face now that he knew of my shame, I covered my face with my hands.

"Ellora, you aren't weak." Macarius nuzzled my neck. "I heard you threaten to cut off a man's balls and wear them.

You didn't have to shift to your human form, but you did because you wanted to defend us. Then you took it further by showing them that they'd not only lost today's fight, but they'd lost you. That's what a warrior queen would've done when looking down on her captured enemies."

Macarius didn't think I was weak. He understood the battle I'd faced going against natural instincts and didn't judge me for doing what I needed to do to survive. Having such a powerful man reaffirm my inner strength helped repair my damaged confidence.

"One minute, I was petting a silky soft bunny, and the next, I had a naked woman straddling my leg." Grabbing my wrists in a single hand, he stretched my arms above my head, and his voice dropped to a husky growl that caused my body to clench with renewed need. "Darling, the raw sexiness you exuded nearly stopped my heart. It took all my control to keep my wolf from taking you on the spot. The only thing stopping me had been my need to know that you wanted me."

"Macarius, the human side doesn't get a say about claiming when being bred during heat. Our shifter latches onto the male, or males, who help us through our heat. She then claims them as her mates." The words tasted bitter on my tongue. "That's what happened during my heat."

"I despise those men, but I will keep myself from killing them if they are your mates. It will be hard to share you with another man, let alone those men, but as long as I am chained when you are with them, we can make it work." The pleading in his eyes broke my heart.

"You would do that for me?" I'd gone from men who were annoyed by my requests to create a nest to having an intimidating predator offer to chain himself if only I would keep him.

"It's more complicated than that. Male rabbits do get a choice, and my matched chose not to claim me in return. Even though our bond wasn't completed, and my inner bunny no longer acknowledges them as her mates, I'm still experiencing the effects of being away from them. I refuse to go back to them, but from what the elders taught us, that means things are going to get worse for me."

Macarius released my wrists and scooted down the bed to rest his cheek against my belly. "How much worse?" he whispered.

"Let's just say I'll be a boss babe running my very own fertilizer and worm bait business before too long." I forced a laugh and tried to push some humor into my tone.

It came across flat, even to myself.

Macarius gave a very dog-like whine. How could he make those sounds in his human form?

"Is there anything we can do?"

"No." Without realizing it, I'd begun to run my fingers through his hair. "Although it's odd. I don't feel as bad when I'm touching you or your brothers. The pain is muffled, and the instincts pushing me to return to my mates are silenced. Do you think it has something to do with the pull I feel toward the three of you?"

Macarius cradled my hips, his face still pressed to my stomach. The intimacy of our positions should have been erotic, but it was strangely comforting. He'd already told me he wanted my body, but instead of getting himself off, he'd been focused on my needs—both the physical and emotional ones.

When he remained silent, I said, "Quin and Coda told me their wolves believe I'm their mate."

The wolf shifter mumbled curses under his breath. "It's going to be hard not to kill them if I see them kissing you."

"That might not be a problem. I told them they can't mark me, because I don't want to risk that I won't be able to claim them back. It would break my heart for them to be left in limbo like my matched did to me." I traced his face with my finger. "You claimed me before I could warn you. I'm so sorry, Macarius."

His thumb rubbed gentle circles on my hip. "Do you want me as your mate?"

"It doesn't matter what I want—"

"All that matters is what you want." Macarius placed slow kisses up my stomach toward my breasts. "If the past was no more, would you want to claim me as your mate? Would you want to have my mark?"

"Yes," I answered with absolute certainty.

Tension drained from Macarius's muscles, a sign of how worried he'd been about what my answer might be.

"Just because I want you to be my mate, it doesn't mean that I can." I clenched the linen blanket in my fist.

"You are the sexiest woman I've ever seen, but you aren't a siren who lured me into making a decision I didn't want. I do not regret my bite, and even with what you've told me, I would claim you again." His mouth brushed along the underside of my left breast. "Even if the claim remains one-sided, it's enough for me to know that you want me as your mate."

Macarius's desire for me was strong enough that he was willing to take whatever scraps I could give him, just to be with me. Status and money didn't even factor into his decision. He didn't want me to be his maid, personal chef, arm candy, or sex toy to use at his whim.

The predator who could kill without breaking a sweat was offering me his heart.

He wanted to belong to me.

My worry over what might happen in the future bled away. The critical voice in my head that said I wasn't worthy of being loved vanished, and the cracks in my soul began to heal.

I was done second-guessing myself and beating myself up for the things I couldn't change. Going forward, I was determined to be the real me—the me who knew her value and fought for what she wanted and deserved.

And what did the new me want to do first? That was simple. I'd already given him a peep show, and now I wanted to go for an Easter egg hunt... in his pants.

# Chapter FOURTEEN

## ELLORA

I f I'd thought my inner bunny was going to be reluctant about getting physical with another man, I would have been wrong. She surged to the surface, not pushing for a shift, but wanting to be as close to his wolf as possible.

His mouth sucked and teased my breasts until my nipples were hardened peaks, and I was writhing beneath him.

"Macarius," I begged, arching my back off the bed and trying to wrap my legs around him to pull him against me.

The frustrating man continued to lavish attention on my breasts. "There is no need to rush. Let me please you."

I growled in both pleasure and displeasure. "Then will you please take off these pants and let me guide you down my magic rabbit hole?"

Macarius's laugh was low and caused the lust building

in my stomach to coil tighter. "Did you seriously just make a white rabbit joke?"

"Yes." I bit the inside of my cheek to keep from laughing. "Did it work?"

"No." Macarius trailed kisses between my breasts and up my neck.

Snarling, I bit his shoulder. It wasn't hard enough to break the skin, but hard enough to make my point. I was soaked, and my body ached with the need for release. Since it was his fault, he needed to fix it.

Macarius pressed a kiss to my temple, not even wincing at my bite. "Ellora, I need to make sure you are relaxed and your body is ready for me."

The hesitation in his voice and the way his eyes didn't meet mine caused my heart to twist in worry. "We can stop if you don't want to do this," I offered, wondering if he'd changed his mind.

Macarius's chocolate brown eyes glowed a bright gold, then he pushed me back on the bed and his teeth dug into the skin of my throat. "We want this—more than we should. You are in danger."

His voice echoed as though two voices had been layered on top of each other.

"That's old news. I've been in danger for a while." Sinking my fingers into his hair, I pulled him tighter to my throat. "At least this is the fun kind of danger."

His left hand moved to knead my breast as his tongue lapped at my throat. "You should run, little rabbit," the gravelly voice warned.

Who was he kidding? Things were just getting good. "No."

Macarius shifted onto his knees. All gentleness gone, he roughly grabbed my hips and ground me against his erection. "Do you feel that?"

Even through his pants, I could feel the heat of his erection. My eyelids fluttered closed, and I moaned in ecstasy.

"Run. Please." His words were stilted.

Opening my eyes, I took in the strain on his face. He was fighting to remain in control, but it was a battle he wasn't going to win. All I needed to do was to push him a little.

"Maybe you should run. Wolves are known for their huffing, puffing, and eating grandmas. But do you know what bunnies are known for?" I smirked up at the mountain of a man who'd continued to grind me slowly along his rigid length. "Easter, energy, and sex. Lots and lots of sex. That's why it's called breeding like bunnies."

Macarius's tongue slid along his bottom lip as he considered my words. "My wolf isn't like other wolves. He's unstable. Even if you were a wolf female, I wouldn't trust myself with you."

I snorted. "Rabbits have the entire world fooled with the cute and cuddly act. We are savages by nature, and if we were the size of wolves, the world would tremble in terror of us."

His breathing had grown ragged, and the worry in his glowing eyes was bleeding into hunger. Lowering my hips to the bed, he crouched over me, his muscles flexing.

I just needed to push him a little more. "Do you think I

haven't been hurt during sex? Bruises, marks, and sprains were common after being with my matched."

"They hurt you?" Macarius snarled, a mask of rage settling on his face.

Although he was in his human form, it reminded me of the hellhound of a wolf who rescued me. I'd watched the small, horse-sized wolf take down the red wolves with unsettling ease.

He was right. If I were smart, I would hop my cotton-tailed butt away from here. But I wasn't afraid of him. Knowing what lurked inside him, eager to protect and please me, I'd never felt safer.

"I'll be back." Macarius rose from the bed and strode toward the door.

"What?!" Scrambling after him, I grabbed the waistband of his slacks. "Where are you going?"

"Hunting," he answered, not even slowing as he continued toward the door.

"You can't leave me hot and needy!" I growled, moving in front of him to block his path to the door.

"My hunt won't take long." Picking me up, he set me to the side like I weighed nothing.

"Fine." Running past him, I reached for the doorknob. "I'll go find Coda and ask him to finish what you started."

His arm circled my waist and strode to the bed. He tossed me onto the mattress, and I watched with growing anticipation as he unbuttoned his pants and let them fall to the floor.

I didn't get much time to enjoy the view before he was

on top of me, his weight pressing me into the mattress and his lips mere millimeters from mine. "If you intend to take my brothers as lovers, I will do my best to keep from killing them. But it would be wise not to goad me, since sharing does not come naturally to me."

It was hard, but I managed to keep a grin from spreading across my face. "Noted. But it would be wise for you to remember my kind has a sex drive that is so legendary, they even named a sex toy after us. The real question is, can my wolf mate keep up?"

I didn't know if it was the challenge or me calling him my mate, but one of them caused all Macarius's reservations to melt away. His fingers brushed the length of my slit before delving inside.

I whimpered as he stretched me, preparing my body to take him. My need for release coiled tighter with each stroke of his fingers until I couldn't tell if I was experiencing pleasure or pain.

His fingers disappeared, leaving me on the verge of release and frustrated. I opened my mouth to complain, but snapped it closed when the head of his cock pressed against my entrance.

"Are you ready?" His voice was husky.

"I've been ready." I narrowed my eyes. "You're the one who keeps stalling."

Macarius shifted forward, filling me until I was sure I couldn't take another inch. But thanks to my rabbit shifter anatomy, my body had been designed to adjust itself for breeding. As he continued to bury himself deeper, my tight channel warmed, stretching and melding itself to accommodate his erection.

"Your body fits around me like a glove, like you were made for me." Sweat beaded Macarius's brow.

He slowly pulled his hips back and then rocked forward. Neither of us spoke as his pace grew faster and harder with each thrust.

His mouth placed kisses across my skin, and his fingers explored every inch of my body he could access without breaking his rhythm. All the while, Macarius watched my face, searching for signs of discomfort and hints at what I enjoyed.

I'd believed sex was just sex, and how my matched felt about me hadn't changed the basics of the act. But I'd been very, very wrong. Being with Macarius was like experiencing it for the first time.

I couldn't hide my smile as I thought about how things might be if I survived to my next heat. He was going to lose it when the heat turned me into living candy.

When I'd left my burrow, I hadn't expected to have sex again. But now I found myself hoping I survived long enough to experience a heat with my wolf—or wolves.

How strange that rabbit females dreaded their heat and the side effects that came with it, but I was looking forward to watching how the wolves reacted to the changes that were meant to make a female rabbit irresistible to her mates.

The pain of separation had dulled to the point I couldn't

feel it, and my inner beast was very eager to mate with this man. Again and again.

Those two things made me question what I'd been taught by the elders. Maybe there could be a future for me far away from the burrows and the men I'd been matched with.

Wrapping my arms around Macarius's neck, I clung to him as a tiny seedling of hope took root in my chest. Even if my rabbit couldn't claim him and complete the mate bond, this man was mine.

On impulse, I darted out my tongue and licked his chest.

Macarius leaned his head back to study my face but still continued to stroke himself inside me, pushing us toward our climax. "What was that?"

My first instinct was to avert my gaze, but that was the old me. Instead, I grinned at him. "I licked you, so now you're mine, and I'm keeping you."

"Is that so?" Amusement shimmered in his golden eyes.

I brushed the back of my fingers over his short beard. "Yes. That's the way these things work."

Macarius stilled and caught my bottom lip between his teeth. "Keep me forever."

"I plan to." Kissing his mouth, I pulled back and scowled. "Although I might change my mind if you keep stalling."

He didn't say a word but flipped our positions so that I was on top and he was beneath me. His erection was buried deep inside me, its heat branding my insides.

I'd never ridden on top of a man, and when I shifted my hips against him for the first time, I moaned in ecstasy. This position provided friction and caused his length to stroke me in amazing new ways.

"Now who's stalling?" Macarius teased.

His hands once again gripped my hips, and he began to rock me against him. As he moved faster, my climax built at an alarming pace.

My muscles clenched around him. Macarius responded with a growl and thrust his hips up against me.

"Macarius," I moaned his name as stars sparkled in my vision. "I'm going to—"

His left hand left my hip, and he rubbed his thumb against my clit. It pushed me over the edge, and I screamed his name as my orgasm made it impossible to think, see, or even breathe. All I could do was ride the endless waves of pleasure.

With each aftershock, my muscles tightened around his cock.

"HADES!" Macarius gasped. "What is happening?"

He bucked hard against me, his eyes glazed with lust.

My body was literally milking the orgasm from him, but I couldn't tell him that since I still couldn't remember how to speak.

It didn't matter, because with the next thrust, his muscles tightened, and he roared my name. I stared down at Macarius, and my chest warmed. He was the first man to mark me as his.

When the aftershocks ended, I slid off Macarius. Unsure

what to do, I sat beside him on the edge of the bed. He rose from the bed and disappeared into a small washroom that was connected to his bedroom.

He returned to the bed with a warm, wet cloth. Kneeling on the floor in front of me, he used the cloth to wipe away the sticky evidence of our lovemaking.

"I need you to open your thighs, darling."

Unable to believe what he was doing, I parted my thighs a bit wider. I was exposed to him, but I was too caught off guard to be embarrassed as Macarius gently cleaned me.

When he finished, his hands moved to my leg that had been bitten by the rogue. The wounds had closed, but the skin around the bite mark had turned a dark plum color, and the swelling hadn't gone down. It would be healed by morning.

Once he finished inspecting my calf, his eyes moved up my body. Regret flashed across his face when he caught sight of the marks that had been left by his fingers digging into my hips. Leaning forward, he placed a tender kiss over each mark.

"They will be gone within hours." I hated for him to be upset over marks he'd left during the height of our passion. Besides, I knew he'd wear marks from my nails and teeth if he helped me through my next heat. "Feel free to let your wolf play a bit rougher next time."

"I'll consider it." He brushed his lips against mine and stood.

After depositing the cloth into the laundry basket, he lay

down on the bed on his side. We remained quiet for several minutes before he spoke.

"Is something wrong?" His brow was creased as he searched my face.

"I'm not sure what I'm supposed to do now." My stomach clenched uncomfortably.

Raising himself onto his left elbow, he reached out with his right hand to play with a strand of my hair. "What do you normally do?"

"Usually, the men visited my room when they had, um, well, needs..." I swallowed hard. "When they finished, they left."

"I don't understand." Macarius shook his head. "Are you saying they didn't share a bed with you? You were left alone?"

I nodded.

He gathered me into his arms. "Never again. I want you in my arms, and in our bed, every night for the rest of our lives."

I couldn't help the happy tears that slid down my cheeks and splashed onto his bare chest.

Macarius settled us back onto the bed and tucked the blanket around me. "Sleep well, little mate."

# Chapter FIFTEEN

## ELLORA

"You better open this door and let us in!" Coda's angry shouts roused me from sleep.

"Not by the hair of your chinny chin chin," Macarius mumbled, his voice husky with sleep.

At my giggle, he cracked open one eyelid to look at me. Seeing I was awake, his arm snaked around my waist and pulled me close.

I pressed my body against him and rested my cheek on his bare chest. "It's even better than I imagined."

"What's even better, pet?" He kissed the top of my head, and his hand snuck down to cup my bare butt.

"Snuggling." I tilted my head so I could look up at him. "And sharing a bed with my mate."

Macarius held me tight, and I thought I heard him whisper something about murder. "We'll take you to the store so you can get whatever you want for the house to make you more comfortable. I'm not sure what type of sheets and blankets you prefer."

"We can hear that you're awake! Open the door before we take it down." Quin hit the door hard enough that it shook.

"I'm enjoying a morning with my mate. Can I ignore you another time?" Macarius called.

He gave me a wicked grin and slid his hand up along my rib cage until he could cup my breast. I had a decent pair of sweater pups, but his massive palms dwarfed them.

When his mouth found mine, the rest of the world ceased to exist.

"You taste even sweeter this morning," Macarius groaned, and his thumb teased my nipple. He swallowed my moan of pleasure.

I was so lost to his touch that I didn't notice Quin and Coda had entered the bedroom until a second pair of hands slid across my bare skin.

Yelping in surprise, I rolled over to find Coda had laid down behind me. "Hi?"

"Good morning, sexy." The sheet was pooling at my waist, and Coda's eyes traveled down my body.

Macarius hauled me back against his chest and rumbled a warning. "Mine."

Coda set his jaw. "Monroe gave her to Quin and me. You will not take her from us."

Speaking of Quinten, his dark wolf leaped onto the bed. The overgrown dog crawled up the bed and decided to lie right on top of me, burying me under his fur.

He could have smothered me with the weight of his large frame, but he managed to keep the bulk of his weight off me. I tried to wrap my arms around his middle to hug him, but I couldn't reach all the way around his body.

"Are you an idiot? Get off her!" Macarius roared.

The wolf tilted his head to the side and looked down at my face between his front legs.

"You're adorable!" I cooed, scratching at his sides.

The wolf snorted, and I got the impression he didn't like being called adorable. Dropping his head, Quin licked my face.

"You licked me, so does that mean I'm yours?" I asked, remembering that I'd licked Macarius the night before.

"He's in his wolf form. It doesn't count," Macarius growled.

A heartbeat later, the wolf disappeared, and I found myself pinned under Quin's human body.

His very naked body.

I blinked in shock, my caffeine-deprived mind struggling to make sense of the abrupt change.

Quin moved fast, pressing his lips to mine in a passionate kiss. When I gasped in surprise, he used it as an opportunity to explore the heat of my mouth. His tongue teased mine, stirring up the lust that seemed to be ever-present when I was with these three.

Releasing my mouth, Quin asked, "I've licked you. Does that make you mine?"

"Yeah, sure?" I whispered, still reeling from his kiss and wishing he'd do it again.

"Good," Quin grinned.

Macarius hauled Quin away from me with a snarl. "Ellora wears my mark. She's my mate."

His muscles trembled, and the odd double-layered voice was back. I couldn't believe they were taking the silly licking thing so seriously.

"Guys, let's not do this." I kept my voice calm. Pushing myself into a sitting position against the headboard, I tried to reason with them. "Macarius, we talked about this last night. You were going to try not to kill them?"

"But I want to," he answered, as though it was a legit option.

"Try it," Quin snarled, pushing himself up off the mattress and readying to fight. "I don't want to share her any more than you do. But she accepted you as a mate, so I will learn to tolerate another male touching her."

While Macarius and Quin were busy having a werewolf dick-measuring contest, Coda positioned himself in front of me.

Feeling exposed, I went to cover my chest with the sheet, but Coda gently freed it from my grasp and slid it even farther down my body.

My body flushed as his eyes took in my bare skin. His eyes darkened and locked with mine. Without breaking eye contact, he gently parted my legs. My breathing became erratic as I waited to see what he would do next.

In a smooth move, he dipped his head between my thighs and ran his tongue along my slit.

"Coda!" I moaned and gripped the bedsheet to keep

from coming up off the mattress at the intense sensations he was causing.

My moan must have caught Macarius's attention, because one minute, Coda was between my thighs, and the next, Macarius pinned him against the wall by his throat. How could he move so fast? It was unsettling.

"Macarius! Put him down!" I ordered, trying to sound confident.

The larger wolf looked between Coda and me, struggling with the desire to please me or the desire to give in to his possessiveness. His glowing eyes softened as he looked at me, and he lowered his arm.

The moment his grip on Coda's neck eased, the idiot decided to press his luck. "I knew she was mine from the moment I saw her at the alpha's house. But I was reminding her that I've licked her, so she's mine too. And when she allows it, I will mark her as my mate. None of us have talked about the possibility of sharing a mate, but we aren't willing to walk away from her. Our only option is to learn how to share without trying to kill each other."

Quin sat on the end of the bed, his muscles flexing as he prepared to jump in and separate the wolves if needed.

Coda wasn't finished. "Do you think it was easy for Quin and me to leave you alone with her last night? We cleaned up the mess you made in the bathroom and dealt with the alpha, all the while knowing our mate was alone with your feral wolf."

"We knew coming in could set off your wolf and Ellora might end up hurt, so we had to listen for any signs that you'd lost control in case she needed us. That means we heard every whimper and moan she made as you pleasured her. I was rock hard and angry all night thanks to that special kind of torture." Coda leaned back against the wall and crossed his arms over his chest.

"I'm so sorry." Guilt weighed heavy on my soul, and I buried my face in my hands. "Rabbit shifter males don't feel jealousy with each other. This was too much to ask of you three."

All three men rushed to sit beside me or kneel in front of me.

"You didn't ask us to share. Coda and I knew the night we brought you home that our wolves weren't willing to give you up. That meant we had to learn to share. Simple as that." Quin caught my hand in his and gave it a gentle squeeze.

"This is our problem, not yours. Many wolves live in harems, it just wasn't something we had planned for. But we'll adjust." Coda sat on the floor in front of me and rested his chin on my knees. "Hades! I alternated between wanting to knock down the door to kill Macarius for touching you, to wishing I could be in the room and watch your face as he made love to you. With time, our wolves will realize they don't have to be so possessive, because you belong to all three of us."

Macarius sat beside me, staring down at the floor. "My wolf isn't the same as the rest of the wolves in the pack. He's wild, untamed, and makes decisions on instinct. He will learn to accept our dynamic as your—what did you call it?"

I rested my head against his arm and smiled. "In the burrow, we call it a fluffle. But we can call it our pack or family."

Macarius kissed the top of my head. "No, my wolf and I are proud to be part of your true fluffle. I will need you three to be patient with us until I can learn to control his possessiveness. It's one thing to say we're sharing, but seeing another man's tongue tasting my mate is going to take some getting used to."

"Why put yourselves through this?" I asked. "I don't have a choice about having a fluffle. During her heat, the female rabbits can literally breed their mates to death. The elders match us with a fluffle so the men can take turns resting. But you could each find a girl who isn't a bunny, and who doesn't have a killer sex drive. Then you wouldn't need to stress your wolves or yourselves."

"Wolves pick their mates and claim them. We aren't forced into arranged matches by our alpha. Our wolves picked you. They will do anything on earth to have you, and we will do anything within our power to make you happy and protect you." As he spoke, Coda inspected the barely visible bite marks on my calf.

"Our wolves want to please you, and once they realize we can bring you more pleasure by working together, they will be excited to work together to drive you wild." Quin kissed the back of my hand and dropped his voice to a whisper. "There were several times last night when my wolf wanted to come join the fun. He'll come around."

"You mentioned heat the night we told you we wanted you as our mate. What does it mean?" Coda asked, his hands sliding down my calf to massage my foot.

"Oh, yeah. I guess I didn't explain that." After the intimacy of our conversation, telling them about my heat shouldn't be embarrassing. So why was I struggling with it? "It's very much exactly what it sounds like. Female rabbits don't experience a heat cycle, but rabbit shifters do."

Taking a steadying breath, I plunged ahead. "During my heat, my body will be driven by the need to breed. I will be in pain, and if I ignore it and refuse to breed, it will continue to get worse. The heat makes a female shifter desperate to be mounted and bred, thus ensuring our species will continue to survive."

When I grew quiet, Quin asked, "What if a female rabbit continues resisting?"

I couldn't meet his eyes. "We die."

"We won't let you die, Ellora," Coda swore

"Pet, you are acting like it will be a burden to care for you." Macarius caught my chin between two fingers and turned me to face him.

"I don't think you understand!" I snapped, frustrated that he wasn't getting it. "This isn't a normal level of need. With my first heat, I hated my matched and fought my needs as much as possible. Yet, they were exhausted and needed time to recover after my heat. I didn't desire them.

So imagine how bad it will be for you three when I want you so bad it hurts when I'm not in heat!"

"I can't wait to find out," Macarius purred, brushing his lips against mine.

Throwing up my hands, I growled in frustration. "Yeah, let's see if you're still enjoying it when I've ridden you until you're raw, but you feel like you can't tap out because I'm still curled up in pain. Or when you are awakened from a much-needed nap by my begging, or you're trying to eat and I'm humping your leg in my sleep. My matched were sick of dealing with my needs by the time the heat ended."

"That's why you needed wolves, my love. Rabbit shifter boys can't compete with the stamina of wolf shifter men. You can take as much as you need from us, and we will still be eager to give you more." Macarius caught my lips in a searing kiss that kept me from responding.

I don't know what would have happened if the alpha hadn't sent a mental message to the guys. He asked us to come to his house in thirty minutes to discuss developments with my burrow.

I rushed to shower, find clothes, and brush the tangles from my hair. All the while, my stomach churned like a toy boat caught in a whirlpool. Would they make me go back?

I watched the men I considered my mates, even if it wasn't official. There was no way I could leave them. I belonged to them—body and heart.

# Chapter SIXTEEN

## ELLORA

"If you don't want to go, we will handle it. Ellora, remember that you don't have to do anything you don't want to." Monroe leaned toward me, compassion shimmering in her eyes.

I looked down at my hands and tried to figure out how I should handle this mess. The thing I'd been dreading most had happened.

My parents had arrived in town, and after they were refused access onto pack-owned land, they'd switched to demanding a meeting with me.

And according to pack security, they hadn't come alone. They'd brought their personal attorney and a representative from the elders.

Cillian sighed. "There's one more thing, Ellora. I had the cops meet me at the house last night and took all four rabbit shifters into custody. But they were bailed out this morning as soon as the courts opened."

"I should have killed them," Macarius snarled, tightening his arms around me.

"No, you did the right thing. Things would've gotten really messy if you'd killed them," Cillian assured him.

Macarius shrugged. "They broke into my house. It would have been self- defense."

Cillian barked a laugh. "Mac, we both know every single wolf shifter in America would turn tail and run rather than face you in a fight. If predators refuse to stand up to you, no one would believe that rabbit shifters caused you to fear for your life."

"I wasn't afraid for my life, but I was terrified for Ellora's life." Macarius nuzzled my neck, pausing to breathe my scent into his lungs.

Rig sat on the couch with his arm around Monroe. "I would've helped kill them if you'd called me instead of Cillian."

Monroe rolled her eyes at him. "We're well aware of that fact, Rig."

When Monroe looked away, Rig pretended to hold a phone up to his ear and mouthed 'call me' to Macarius.

"He's as unhinged as you are," I whispered to Macarius.

"Yeah, Rig and I have made some great memories over the years." A lazy smile spread across my mate's face.

His sexiness had my ovaries swooning. It was crazy to think that when I lived in the burrow, I never imagined that bad boys were my type.

There was something about men who could make everyone else in the room tremble in fear that made a girl feel protected. Not to mention the thrill I got every time their wolf instincts surfaced, and they got possessive over me.

I'd gone from being ignored unless I needed to satisfy the rabbit shifters' sexual or physical hunger to having three men who couldn't get enough of me. They kept finding reasons to touch me or brush against me, as though reassuring themselves I was safe while reminding me I wasn't alone.

Pulling my mind back to the problem at hand, I tapped my fingers on the arm of the chair. "Cillian? Is it possible they'll show up at the meeting my parents have set up?"

The alpha nodded. "I'd say it's very likely they'll be there. My wolves are following them, so I'll know before you arrive if they're in that vicinity."

"You could always tell your parents you don't want to meet now. I'm guessing you're eager to put this behind you, but maybe you should put it off for a few days so you can rest," Monroe suggested.

That was exactly what I wished I could do. Plus, I would've loved to put them off if for no other reason than to inconvenience them.

But getting the meeting over with today was for the best, because there was something I hadn't shared with the group.

My heat was coming.

I thought I would've had more time before it hit, but

maybe the stress of leaving the burrows and everything that had happened since I showed up on Monroe's doorstep had brought it on sooner.

Just since waking up that morning, I'd noticed the changes had begun. My breasts were becoming fuller, and my skin was glowing.

I could have chalked those up to finally being happy, but then the men's kisses on my skin began to linger as they licked up the hint of sweetness I'd begun to exude. In the past hour, all three men had found a reason to smell me.

My last heat had hit me hard and fast, not giving me a chance to ease into it. And the last thing I wanted was to go into my second heat stressing out over what my ex-matched and parents were plotting.

Blowing out the breath I'd been holding, I made my decision. "I'll do it, but tell them I will stay for half an hour and not a minute more."

Monroe grinned. "I like the way you think!"

She hurried out of the room to accept the invitation to the meeting, and feeling relieved the decision was made, I sagged against Macarius.

"It will be over soon, my love."

Actually, the real trouble would start soon. He didn't know it, but the meeting was going to be a cakewalk compared to the strenuous demands of my heat.

I was like an Easter bunny, sweet but hollow on the inside... but if my heat got its way, soon I would be a cream-filled bunny.

AN HOUR LATER, we stepped out of the elevator onto the twenty-fifth floor of a downtown hotel in the neighboring city. The hotel had been built near the airport and catered to businessmen who flew into town and needed to hold meetings during their stay.

Cillian hadn't been pleased about us having the meeting there because it was owned by humans, and he had less control over who could come and go from the hotel. I thought he was overreacting a bit, though.

I was being escorted by Macarius, Coda and Quin. And while I was in the meeting, Cillian, Monroe, Rig and Syrus were patrolling around the hotel.

After their plan to kidnap me failed so spectacularly, I doubted they would work up the courage to try again. They didn't really want me. All they cared about was regaining the power and control they felt they lost and saving face within the burrow.

Reaching the conference room door, Quin opened it and allowed me to enter first. I walked in to find my mother and father sitting at the head of the table as though they were about to hold court.

A gentleman I vaguely recalled seeing at the elder meeting sat on my mother's right-hand side, and my family's beady-eyed attorney sat on my father's left side.

I moved toward the opposite end of the table and

paused. Unlike the plush office chairs my parents were using, the chairs at our end of the table looked like they'd been in use for longer than I'd been alive.

I immediately recognized one of my parents' favorite intimidation tactics. These chairs lacked the levers that adjusted their height. It wouldn't be a problem for my wolves, but my diminutive height was going to make me look like a sixth grader.

They wanted me to feel like a naughty child who was being scolded by authority figures. I kept my face emotionless, but tried to decide how best to handle the situation.

The three wolves took their seats first, and I knew instantly what I would do. Calling on my newly found confidence, I took a seat on Macarius's lap. The corner of his mouth twitched, but otherwise, he showed no reaction.

Sitting on his thighs added significantly to my height, and I struggled to hide my grin at the anger flashing across my mother's face.

"Your thirty minutes starts now." Interlacing my fingers, I lifted my chin and eyed my parents with cool disinterest.

"How are we supposed to take you seriously right now? I never expected my daughter to become the purse pet of an ill-tempered beast." My mother's nostrils flared. It was a small detail, but it told me I'd gotten under her skin.

It was amusing how close to the truth she'd hit, though. I wouldn't be surprised if Macarius showed up with a purse to carry me around in. I'd barely convinced him to set me down before we entered the hotel.

"I think you've misread the situation." Macarius's voice

was smooth as honey, but laced with venom. "I'm Ellora's pet. Eager to do her bidding and find ways to please her."

His words and the underlying innuendo unleashed a wave of raw lust through my blood. The temperature in the room seemed to rise several degrees, and a thin sheen of sweat coated my body.

Tiny lightning bolts of fiery pain sizzled through my body. My heat was growing in strength and I wasn't ready for it. Not yet.

"Is that a mate mark on your neck?" My father adjusted his glasses and peered at my neck.

"Yes." I'd purposely styled my long hair to leave my neck bare so they could see the mark.

"You claimed another mate after your first heat? This complicates things." The scrawny man scribbled notes on a pad of paper. "The elders will be displeased."

Technically, my rabbit hadn't completed the bond, but he didn't need to know that. I leaned forward. "What do you mean the elders will be displeased?"

"Historically, female rabbits have only been able to take mates after their first heat if the original mates were found lacking." The man shoved his gold-rimmed eyeglasses up his nose and continued to make notes. "If word spreads about this, it could damage the reputation of four of our finest families. This will need to be handled quickly."

"So this is proof that Ellora's matched mates failed her." Quin drummed his fingers on the table and smiled like the cat that caught the canary. "And now you're going to try to cover it up?"

"Yes— I mean, no!" the man stammered. "This is a rare situation, and it's best for the burrows to handle it quietly."

"Because you would rather blame Ellora than admit she was used as a chess piece for personal gain by her parents, her matched, and the elders?" Coda's face was calm, but a hurricane brewed in his eyes.

The old man opened and closed his mouth like a fish out of water but couldn't spit out a single sentence. What could he say when Coda had nailed the situation?

Turning to look at Macarius, I asked, "How many minutes are left, my love?"

His eyes glowed for a moment at the word love, and then he tapped his phone screen to check the time. "Twenty-two more minutes."

"I'm afraid it is going to take quite a bit longer to go over these documents." The lawyer laid a manilla folder on the table and pulled out a stack of papers.

I smiled at the lawyer. "You have twenty-one minutes before we walk out that door, so you should make them count."

# Chapter SEVENTEEN

## ELLORA

"Ellora! Stop being rude. You will sit here until we sort out this childish mess you have made," my father scolded me.

My mother rubbed her forehead as though she felt a migraine coming on. "Why couldn't you just do as you were told? They didn't beat you, they kept you alive during your heat, and you lived in the most exclusive neighborhood in Greenbriar. What more could you have possibly wanted?"

"It would have been nice if my matched would have allowed me to build a nest for my heat, but they denied my request for fear it would hurt Clarice's feelings." I dig my fingernails into my palms beneath the table, determined not to cry. "I was allowed to pick three pillows and a blanket. That was it."

Macarius's muscles flexed beneath me while Coda and Quin stared at me with twin expressions of heartbreak.

"You threw away the reputation your father and I spent decades building because you could only have two pillows?" My mother flattened her palms on the table and glared at me. "You selfish little brat."

"No! I stayed, even after they forced me to go through my first heat in a house that smelled like another woman. I stayed even after they refused to complete the bond and claim me as their mate. I stayed even after crying myself to sleep every time they got their rocks off and left me alone. I stayed even after I realized they wanted me to show me off for brownie points with their bosses, but wanted to ignore my existence until the next time they needed to use me for their own selfish purposes." My breathing was coming in harsh pants, and a violent cramp twisted my uterus.

I nearly passed out from the sudden pain, but somehow, Macarius sensed my pain, and his hand slid beneath my shirt to rest low on my stomach. At the skin-to-skin contact, the cramp loosened, and I was able to take a deep breath.

My mother remained oblivious to my pain. "It sounds like you expected to be treated like a princess and didn't like having to earn your keep."

I thought I was long past my mother being able to hurt me, but my heart ached at her words. "You never loved me, did you?"

My parents avoided my gaze.

"Ellora, I think therapy would be a better place to have this discussion with your parents?" The lawyer slid a paper toward me. "I'd like you to look at this so you're aware of the consequences you face for breaching the matched contract. That might help you understand how precarious your position is and how patient your parents and your matched are to give you a chance to return and make things right."

His smug face was the final straw.

Ignoring the paper, I told him the truth. "I'd rather swan dive into a pool filled with lava than stay in this room another minute."

My father stood and glared at me. "Ellora! I don't think you understand. If you walk out that door with your mutts, we will sue you, and you will face prison time for breach of contract. We won't show mercy just because you're our daughter."

I rose as well. "You've never treated me as your daughter, and now I know the truth. So here is my counter offer. I'm going to walk out that door and you are never going to contact me again. Not you two, not my matched, their parents, the elders, or anyone else from Greenbriar."

Fiery pain scorched my insides, and I leaned against the table to keep my legs from giving out. I had to hurry this up, or I was going to go into full-blown heat in that awful room. "If you contact me, I will tell everyone the truth about how you only had me so you could make a marriage contract with your friends. The very same contract you are threatening to sue me over breaching. How do you think people will react when they find out you signed that contract yourself while I was still a baby?"

My parents' faces had paled. But I wasn't done.

"Maybe I'll write a tell-all best-selling novel." I tapped my chin. "I bet the chapter discussing how the elders accepted a bribe to match me with the men you wanted will be extra juicy. So much for the elders matching based on compatibility, huh? I guess I didn't deserve the benefits and protection the burrows claim they give to all residents?"

"You can't!" the elder's henchman protested.

"Oh, but I can. And I will." I barely kept from wincing as I stood up straight and eyed them each in turn. "And I have a message for my exes. Tell them if they go against me and try anything, I will tell their bosses, their colleagues, and every single female bunny in the burrows the truth."

I took a moment to swallow the emotion clogging my throat before continuing. "How will their reputations hold up when people find out that my last night in Greenbriar, I was awakened by the sounds of another woman being pleasured in my mate's bedroom in what was supposed to be our home? I won't forget to share how the following morning, I watched as that same female waltzed into the dining room in a robe to eat the food I'd prepared… while sitting on my mate's lap."

They stared at me, wide-eyed and slack-jawed. Focusing on my mother, I whispered, "I left because I realized they would never love me. That's what they didn't give me. Love."

"How did I raise such a fool?" My mother spat the words at me.

"Never contact me again." I turned away from them and

took a step toward the door, only to be hit with a wave of dizziness that caused the room to tilt wildly.

Quin lifted me into his arms and carried me out the door. From somewhere behind us, I heard Macarius speak in his stilted, rough as whiskey voice that meant his wolf was speaking with him.

"My mate is tenderhearted, and it is one of the traits I adore most about her. But let me add the part she didn't mention. If you contact her again, not only will she tear your reputation to shreds, but you will find out just how much my wolf loves violence. Ellora can control him with her touch, but if you don't take her offer, not even she will be able to stop him from hunting you down and sending your souls straight to hell."

The moment we were out of sight of the conference room, I curled into Quin's chest and sobbed.

"Ellora? What's wrong?" Coda appeared at Quin's side.

"I thought I had more time." My words were muffled by Quin's shirt.

Quin stopped walking. "More time for what? Are you dying?"

"Where's that incredible smell coming from?" Macarius asked, sniffing the air.

"Me," I whispered.

All three men leaned forward to breathe in my scent, and in unison, they released a guttural moan.

Coda reached out a hand to touch me, but Quin stepped back and growled.

I whimpered as fire spread through my blood. "I'm in heat. We need to get home before I lose control."

Three sets of hungry eyes stared at me, but no one moved.

"Hurry! Otherwise, we may end up having sex right here in the middle of the hotel, " I growled. "The sooner you get me back to the house, the sooner you'll find out what it's like to breed a bunny in heat."

That last part pulled them from their stupor, and they broke into a full run toward the elevator.

# Chapter
## EIGHTEEN
### ELLORA

**W**e barely made it to the car before the next wave of pain had me curling into the fetal position.

Quin climbed into the back of their sleek SUV and settled me on his lap. "Ellie, how can I help? Please tell me what I can do." His hands moved over my body, trying to comfort me.

There was only one thing that would truly appease the heat enough to ease up, but I wasn't about to ask him to take me right there in the backseat of the vehicle like a horny teenager.

As though my body understood I was delaying getting bred, knife-like pain stabbed my middle. I groaned and tried not to pass out.

"Quin, take off your shirt and hers," Macarius ordered. He was driving, which seemed like a questionable decision since I suspected he would be the one to lose his crap and give in to the call of my heat completely.

Trying his best not to jostle me, Quin pulled his shirt over his head. Moving quickly, he helped me take my shirt off.

"Now what?" Quin asked, stroking his fingers through my hair. "She's burning up!"

"Hold her against you. Try for as much skin-to-skin contact as you can with her. During the meeting, my wolf sensed something was wrong, and he was convinced that would help."

"Tell him thank you," I whispered, blinking hard to clear a wave of dizziness. "It helped a lot."

Quin shifted me in his lap so I sat facing him, with our torsos pressed together. The heat of his skin should have caused me more pain since I was already on fire, but the pain in my abdomen eased ever so slightly.

"Is it helping?" Quin asked.

"Yes," I moaned, thankful to have a brief respite from the pain.

Quin sighed with relief. "Good. We had a bunch of things delivered to the house today for you that we thought you might like for your nest. I'd hoped you would have time to prepare for it, but maybe there will be things you like and we can get anything you're missing."

"What did I do to deserve you three?" I kept my face expressionless as fresh agony twisted my internal organs like cotton candy on a stick.

"We don't deserve you, beautiful girl." Before I could warn him, he kissed my bare shoulder.

We might have made it to the house if it hadn't been for that single kiss.

But once he'd tasted my sugary-sweet skin, it was all over. Like a man starved, Quin sucked his way down my neck and along my collarbone and, sensing a willing male, my heat went into overdrive.

Every inch of my skin became hyper-sensitive and, thanks to the hormones pumping through my body, I was soaked within seconds. When Quin bent and sucked my nipple through the thin fabric of my sports bra, my heat-fueled instincts took over.

Reaching between our bodies, I frantically unbuckled his pants and freed his already stiff length from his pants. As soon as I managed that, I shimmied out of my jeans and thong with a speed that not even Macarius could rival.

"Ellora," Quin hissed, stroking his length as he watched me strip.

Another vicious spasm caused me to dig my nails into his shoulder to keep myself from falling over. "I don't understand why it's so violent this time and why it came on so fast."

Quin responded by pulling the bra over my head so he could lavish attention on my tender breasts. I wanted to close my eyes and savor it, but my body was screaming for more, and it wasn't going to stop until it got what it wanted.

Grabbing his thick erection, I impaled myself in a single

hard movement.

"*Goddess!*" Quin gasped in shock and pleasure.

Blood pounded in my ears, and another wave of sweat coated my body. Grabbing Quin's hands, I guided them to my waist.

"Breed me," I begged, my animal instincts driving me.

He didn't have to be asked twice. Holding onto me, Quin thrust into me with wild abandon and delivering exactly what my body demanded.

I clung to him as his hips moved harder and faster until he sent us both hurtling into orgasmic bliss. That's when it happened.

My rabbit pushed forward, and I knew exactly why my heat was so intense.

She was ready to claim them as ours, and didn't want to wait.

"Mine," I whispered as my rabbit claimed the gorgeous wolf as my mate.

"Yes, I'm yours, Ellie." Quin's eyes glowed with pride as he realized what had happened. "You claimed me. I can sense the bond."

Moving my hair to the side, I tilted my neck. "And I'm yours."

His teeth sank into my neck, marking me as his and completing the mate bond between us.

Instead of easing my heat, Quin claiming me added gasoline to the fire that was my heat. Looking toward the front of the SUV, I was surprised to see we were in our driveway.

When Coda opened the side door, I hopped my naked butt straight into his arms.

He caught me to him and raced inside the house while I worked on undoing his shirt. By the time he got inside, I had his belt off and his shirt unbuttoned.

He sat me down on the back of the couch so he could kick off his pants and boxers. His cock sprung free, and a sharp spasm had me groaning.

"Either breed her and ease her pain or get out of the way!" Macarius snarled. He was standing in the hall, his eyes glowing as he watched.

"Come here," I begged.

"I can't. It is taking every bit of restraint I possess not to rip my brothers apart." Macarius's voice shook, and even in my pain, I longed to ease his stress.

Dropping to my stomach on the back of the couch, I tried not to think about how needy I must appear to present myself to him. I didn't have to worry about Coda's reaction, because the moment I was in position, he was lining the head of his erection up against my entrance.

"Macarius, come to the front of the couch," I whispered.

This time, he gave in and, blurring across the room, sat down close enough that our mouths nearly touched. As Coda pressed himself inside my tight heat, I moaned.

Macarius caught my face between his rough palms and swallowed my sounds of pleasure. Coda's hands traced my spine and the curve of my hips, exploring as he buried himself deeper with his stroke.

The familiar tightening inside me as my orgasm built

had fresh pain rippling through me, along with the bursts of pleasure as my two wolf mates took me higher and higher. Coda moved his hand around my hip and between my thighs. His fingers searched until they located my clit, and I responded by arching my back and bucking.

Coda managed to continue stimulating me while plunging inside me. Macarius's mouth had found my nipples, and when he sucked one of the hardened peaks, my climax tore from me. It mixed with the pain of the heat to create an exquisite pleasure.

"Ellora!" Coda groaned my name as my muscles clenched around his length and forced him to join me in bliss.

I looked at him over my shoulder as my rabbit pushed forward to claim him. "Mine," I whispered as a warm glow warmed my chest.

Coda's hand wrapped around my neck and pulled me toward him until my back was pressed against his chest.

"And you are mine, beautiful bunny." His fangs sank into my neck, completing the bond between us.

My eyes locked with Macarius's glowing golden orbs.

One to go.

Coda had barely removed his fangs from my neck when Macarius pulled me into his arms and blurred us to the bedroom. My back landed on his bed, and I purred in happiness when Macarius wasted no time climbing on top of me and burying his erection in my heat.

"I can't wait any longer, pet. I need you."

I kissed his chest. "I want you every way I can have you.

But right now, I need you to take me hard and fast. We can try gentle when I'm not in heat."

Macarius growled as he plunged himself inside me, angling his hips to stroke me in places I didn't know I possessed.

I was completely lost in the fog of lust and need when Macarius cursed.

Blinking up at him, I watched as his eyes widened with horror.

"No, no, no." He tried to pull away, but I hooked my legs over his hips and held him to me.

"Macarius?"

He kept his eyes closed as though he was using all his energy to concentrate. "You need to be perfectly still. Don't move."

I obeyed, but I wanted answers. "Are you hurt? What's going on?"

"My wolf is pushing to take things too far. Give me a minute to force him to back down."

I snorted. "With my heat calling to him, I don't think he's going to go for that."

"You aren't the only shifter with unusual anatomy, pet." He opened his eyelids and watched me with a hungry gaze.

Curiosity was a heck of a thing.

Licking my lips, I ground myself against him, eager to find out more about what upgrades my wolf mate was trying to hide from me.

"Ellora." Macarius growled the warning, but I didn't miss the way his hands helped me rock myself against him.

I nipped and licked his abs, loving the effect my touch had on him.

His breath hitched, and he dug his fingers into my hips. Once more, he tried to yank me off his cock, but I clamped my thighs tighter around him.

"Ellora! Move!" he commanded me, but no sooner had the words left his mouth than I knew it was too late.

I whimpered in pain as he swelled inside me, stretching me beyond my comfort level and faster than my body could adjust.

"Darling, look at me." When my panicked gaze locked on his face, he spoke again. "It's too late to stop this, but if you trust me and relax, I promise it will feel good."

"I trust you." As I relaxed, the odd round base of his cock slid inside.

Unable to sit still thanks to the heat still driving me to mate, I tentatively rocked my hips. To my surprise, I found that not only were we locked together, but he was pressing against my most sensitive spot.

Gasping with pleasure, I frantically ground against him until a final orgasm rippled through me, quieting the demands of my heat... for now.

"Mark me again, Macarius. Please."

Cradling my head, he placed his teeth over his first bite and claimed me a second time.

"Mine." Warmth spread through me as I claimed my final mate.

Contented and exhausted, I drifted to sleep in my mate's arms.

## ELLORA

"Thanks for inviting us to dinner, Monroe. It was delicious." I patted my stomach and groaned. "Although I'm so stuffed, I don't know if I'll be able to walk home!"

Monroe laughed. "I'm sure Macarius won't mind carrying you. It seems like you've become his emotional support bunny."

Macarius winked at me from where he leaned against the wall. He still wasn't completely comfortable being around people for long stretches of time, but he was doing far better.

"I never thought my brother, the big bad wolf, could be tamed." Reese playfully punched Macarius in the side. "Who knew you were such a softy?"

"Keep that to yourself, sis," Macarius growled, but it was missing any real threat.

"Bro, half the pack has watched you piggy back Ellora around town. Your rep has gone down the drain, but that's on you." Reese snickered and flopped down next to Monroe.

Leaning back against Quin's chest, I sighed happily. I'd escaped a life that had nearly broken me, survived two attempts to make me return to the burrow, and then made it through my second heat. Thankfully I hadn't heard from my old Burrow since the fiasco at the hotel.

Even better, my body was no longer in danger of giving out due to separation. The claims my bunny had made on my ex-matched had faded completely, and the only men she recognized as our mates were Quin, Coda, and Macarius.

I was happy, free, and completely in love with my wolves.

Coda sat down next to Quin on the porch swing and pulled my feet onto his lap. Glancing at Monroe, I saw Syrus was massaging her feet as well.

Wolves were definitely a girl's best friend.

"Who is that?" Cillian stood and moved toward the screened door of the porch with Macarius hot on his heels.

A white rabbit with black spots hopped between the Azalea bushes that lined one side of the property.

The rabbit shifted, and dropped to his knees in front of Cillian.

"Is he from your burrow?" Quin asked me. "If he is, he has signed his death warrant."

I shook my head. "No, there were no spotted rabbits in

the Greenbriar burrow. What about your old burrow, Monroe?"

She shook her head. "I don't recognize him either."

"Why are you on pack land?" Cillian demanded.

The man lifted his hands, trying to show he meant no harm. "I had nowhere else to go, and my matched needs help."

We all scanned the area surrounding the house, but there wasn't another shifter in sight.

Monroe pushed open the screen door and, ignoring Cillian, she crouched in front of the man. "Is she injured? Where is the rest of your fluffle?"

"The men in our fluffle are cruel. She needed to escape, so I helped her run. We'd almost made it here when her heat started, and I can't watch her die!"

A muscle in Monroe's jaw flexed. "So she's suffering because you don't want to be tied to her?"

For the first time, the man lifted his face, and I was shocked to see his eyes were red from crying. "I love her more than my own life and would give anything to claim her, but I thought your pack only offered protection for females who are mistreated by their burrow. Since it's the male shifters who are taking advantage of the females and treating them like crap, I doubted you would welcome me here."

The man grimaced. "Plus, if she claims me during her heat, and I left, she would be in more pain from the separation. I couldn't do that to her. I would rather give her up than have her and see her living under the same roof as those monsters."

"We aren't going to separate you from your love. You are both welcome here and will be under our protection." Cillian offered Monroe his hand and pulled her into his arms. "I'll have several wolves escort you to where you have her hidden and bring her back to pack land."

"And I'll come with you so she doesn't feel outnumbered with so many guys," Monroe offered.

"What about her heat?" The man's green eyes darted back and forth between Cillian and Monroe.

Cillian looked baffled. "What about it? Once you are in a safe house, you can tend to her needs."

"He won't be enough," I whispered, but of course, every wolf heard and looked at me. "Oh, come on! Everyone here should know by now that a lone male would die trying to help a female bunny through her heat."

"Huh. I didn't know that," Reese mused, then a smirk curved her lips. "So you guys don't even need batteries to keep going, and going, going? Or should I say to keep coming, and coming— Ouch!"

Coda tossed a pillow from the porch swing across the room at her. "Enough, brat."

I smiled, but it quickly faded as I thought about the bunny, who was probably terrified and in pain at that very moment.

"Let's get you two safely tucked away on pack land, and then we will figure out the rest." Cillian kept his left arm wrapped around Monroe's waist but offered the man his right hand. "I have an idea, and I've already asked them to head this way through the link."

Standing, I turned to my mates. "If she's in heat, she's going to long for a nest. I went through my first heat without a nest, and I don't want her to have that same experience. I need to go to the store and buy some things for her."

"Then let's go." Quin stood and kissed my cheek.

"I call shotgun for the backseat!" Coda yelled.

"You're supposed to call shotgun if you want the front seat." I rolled my eyes at his weirdness.

Coda leaned close enough that his lips brushed my ear. "But while Quin is driving us to the store, I'm thinking we could enjoy some bunny business in the back seat."

His mouth moved to nibble at the sensitive skin behind my ear, leaving no doubt as to what he had in mind... and I was completely on board with his plan.

I was one very lucky bunny.

# ABOUT SEDONA ASHE

Sedona Ashe doesn't reserve her sarcasm for her books; her poor husband can tell you that her wit, humor, and snarky attitude are just part of her daily life. While she loves writing paranormal shifter reverse harem novels, she's a sucker for true love, twisted situations, and wacky humor.

Sedona lives in a small town at the base of the Great Smoky Mountains in Tennessee. She and her husband share their home with their three children, adorable pup, five cats, two pet foxes, chickens, three crazy turkeys, two cows, and over a hundred reptiles.

When she isn't working, she enjoys getting away from the computer to hike, free dive, travel, study languages, and capture the essence of places and people in her photography. She has a crazy goal of writing one million words in a year and spending six months exploring Indonesia.

www.ingramcontent.com/pod-product-compliance
Lightning Source LLC
Chambersburg PA
CBHW020954180626
46814CB00003B/1085